Macaulay Station

Graeme Sparkes

in case of emergency press

We are proud to acknowledge the Traditional Owners of country throughout Australia and to recognise their continuing connection to land, waters, and culture.

We pay our respects to their Elders past, present, and emerging.

We support recognition, reconciliation, and reparation.

Macaulay Station

Graeme Sparkes

in case of emergency press

http://www.icoe.com.au

Travancore, Victoria

Australia

Published by **in case of emergency press** 2019

ISBN 978-0-9943525-2-1

Acknowledgements

I would like to thank Liz Connell for an early reading of Macaulay Station, Clare Carlin and Rob Watson for their critiques and advice, Helen Cerne, who undertook a thorough appraisal and offered timely encouragement, Michele Gierck, who was like my motivational coach, and my publisher, Howard Firkin, for his insights and enlightened attitude towards publishing.

I would also like to thank my partner, Sonia Gatti, for her patience, candour and the grungy photograph used for the cover.

In memory of Dr Douglas Jordan

Macaulay Station

Table of contents

1	Charlie	1
2	Chloe	87
3	Madonna	90
4	Cliff	106
5	Julia	175
6	Frank	179

1 Charlie

We are in a gloomy corridor of indeterminate length. I feel I've been here all my life. The woman with me wants to take me into a side room whose door is covered in crimson velvet. Who is she? My wife, Julia? My boss, Dukakis, editor-in-chief? She grasps my arm, turns, smiles. Chloe Dukakis! I'm delighted. I've wanted this for a long, long time. An eternity. Is this to be my birthday present? Her opal eyes are glistening and a cigarette hangs from her lips. Despite my professional mien, my heart toils like an old, obsolete, offset press. She says nothing, just blows smoke from the corner of her mouth and motions with her head to lead the way.

The walls of the room are crimson too. There is a bed covered with, of all things, newsprint. And it already supports a naked man. He's on his knees facing us, his thighs atrophied, his mossy nether parts astir, his face familiar; my cantankerous neighbour, the retired Dr Stanley Herbert-Jones, in the papers recently for medical malpractice suits, whose nicotine-stained teeth are set in an optimistic leer. He babbles like a suckling infant but in a timbre borrowed from Vincent Price.

I turn puzzled to Dukakis who draws me out of the way by the shoulder in her haste to enter. But then it's no longer her; it's Julia in her strapless crimson dress, the one she wears to dinner parties, to captivate the philanderers present I suspect. Everything, even the air I'm breathing, appears crimson. I begin to whimper. Then wail. Where has Dukakis gone? Julia shimmies towards the inviting arms of the doctor. While I stare, dismayed, I plead with her. *Not that old creep, surely?* She smirks and nods. I'm flummoxed. Suddenly Julia is gone and Dukakis is back, right in front of me. Unexpectedly—for until this moment we've had an excellent working relationship—she blows smoke into my eyes, flicks her cigarette away, and reminds me she's no longer my boss. I won't be getting a birthday present from the newsroom this year. She laughs aloud, a sudden harsh guffaw that I recognise immediately. My eyes, glued together with sleep, tear open.

It's the wattlebird in reveille on a bough outside our window, which is slightly ajar at Julia's insistence to circulate the air in our room that becomes stale with my nocturnal odours. Each morning these last few weeks, ever since I lost my job, the damn bird has been waking me.

The crimson room and its occupants have vanished. I wait, irresolute, in the haze between sleep and the humdrum of another day.

Light is creeping through the window. Again the loathsome bird calls, as stark as any bugle. I grind my teeth.

Next to me Julia is asleep, snoring softly, her hair dishevelled on the pillow, mascara smudged, clown-like, across her brow and cheeks. Is she still where I was a few moments ago? She stirs and grumbles. I watch her turn. She never gets up as early as I do, not even on my birthday, when one could be forgiven for thinking I'd be entitled to expect breakfast in bed. But I don't blame her. I've always discouraged her enthusiasm for celebrating what I consider another step towards the grave.

Our quilt is a beautiful patchwork affair. Just the look of it is warm and cosy. Julia bought it from an organisation raising money for the homeless. I pull it aside and slip out of bed, sit on the edge, experiencing regret, as usual.

My throbbing head and nausea surprise me, although they shouldn't, not after my star performance at last night's dinner party.

Some light is already creeping through the timber slats of our blinds, sending faint slivers across our copy of a Beardsley print, *The Climax*, hanging in a simple wooden frame on the far wall, which Julia bought soon after we began to live together a few decades ago: Salome, kissing the severed head of John the Baptist. It serves as a constant reminder of female determination and the terror men endure.

The built-in bedroom robe is partially open. I can see her clothes squeezed in, dozens of dresses, pants, blouses, some of them bought just last week, as if she needed more. Some of them I've never seen her wear, or is it that I no longer notice? I can't stop her buying things. She has an independent income after all, while mine is in abeyance.

I place my feet on the carpet. My slippers are there, waiting, pallbearers.

I check the alarm is turned off for her sake. Some nights I turn it on from habit when there is no need. One morning, last week, she complained when it rang unnecessarily. *What's your obsession with routine?* she said, exasperated. *Especially now you have no job. Honestly, Frank, you live like a machine.*

I take a sip from the small glass on the bedside table, next to the lamp and the clock. The water soothes the parched feeling I get in my throat every night. I have a constant irritation that worries me at times, but my GP assures me it's not life threatening, more a low-grade bacterial infection or allergy, probably due to hydrocarbon pollutants in the city air. Now I have some time on my hands, I would like to shift away, do the sea-change or tree-change thing, I don't mind which, but Julia is less keen. She remembers too well our last attempt at country living. Anyway, it's her job, her career and the proximity to friends that will keep us put for the next few years at least, which makes me worry about what condition my throat will be in by the time she is ready to reconsider.

There are other niggling worries too, inexplicable pains that have appeared since my employment was deemed superfluous but don't seem acute enough to speak to the GP about. It's occurred to me that now I'm not working, now I've stopped concentrating on other people's problems, my own have become more apparent. How long have I failed to notice them?

The GP is young enough to be my son. He's probably heard but takes no notice of those maxims I value more each year: *respect your elders, wisdom comes with the years,* etcetera. He usually puts my symptoms down to the ageing process and gives me a lecture, along with recounts of his latest skiing sojourn or the improvement in his golf handicap, on how not so long ago few people lived beyond their fifties. Before the twentieth century life expectancy was much shorter, he informs me, as if my state school education failed me, as if, despite my thirty years as a journalist and avid watching of every health documentary ever shown on TV, this statistic might have eluded me somehow. So we should prepare for a few aches and pains as the body wears out and approaches expiry. *You can blame it on the Enlightenment,* he joked, which makes sense in a convoluted way but is no argument for the return of the Dark Ages. All I want is a reassuring scan. My dear friend, Charlie Johnson, might still be alive if he'd had a scan.

Something hits the window, distracting me, disturbing Julia. The wattlebird? She rolls over and groans but doesn't wake completely. The groan sounds like she's still back in the crimson room enjoying what's on offer there.

Well, let her. She extracts little pleasure out of me these days. Our coupling is much diminished. I'm lucky if we do it once a month. Even then I think she participates out of a sense of duty. The lamentable thing is my sexual desires are no less urgent than they were in my adolescence.

The slippers are still cold. My feet are reluctant intruders. After all, it's footwear bearing me to my funeral, at least part of the way. I rise from the edge of the bed, quietly slip into my dressing gown, which I take from the hook behind the ensuite door where Julia hung it after complaining about me leaving it on a chair. Everything about my dressing gown gives me comfort—its capacious dimensions and weightiness, its tawny hue, its musty smell, the coffee stains on its lapels, the used tissues in its pockets, the errant cord, singed while frying eggs one morning, the fraying hem—it's like slipping into character each morning. I make my way towards the passage, glancing back to ensure she's still sleeping when I almost trip on her crimson dress discarded after the dinner party. Muttering about pots and kettles, I leave the bedroom.

Even though it's my birthday, I'll wake her in half an hour with toast and freshly squeezed orange juice to remind her how magnanimous I can be. Sometimes I need reminding, myself.

Touching my morning erection, which is deconstructing rapidly, I pass through the open bedroom door. I squeeze and release, squeeze and release, as if I'm performing a medical procedure, trying to keep it alive until the paramedics arrive. A bit of genital CPR. It fails to respond and there's no sign of an ambulance. I let it lapse into a coma. Maybe it will need to be put on life support.

I have a study downstairs, tucked away in a quiet corner of the house, where I like to retreat and write or use the internet. It's my study but Julia occasionally occupies it, which I resent, which I consider an insensitive incursion, although she is totally unaware that it offends me or I'm sure she would be more circumspect. She's not a psychopath. She's not on the autism spectrum. She doesn't lack empathy. At times she has too much of it, in my opinion, spending hours—days—weeks—trying to solve the problems of her friends and even near strangers, rather than focusing on her own issues, of which there are plenty, chronic enough to deserve her full attention. Like her obsession with shopping, although most would consider this unremarkable, or her casual approach to schedules.

At times it exasperates me. I hate being late to anything. I know punctuality doesn't bother a lot of people, who make lame jokes about being *fashionably late* to excuse their inconsiderateness, but it bothers me. If three decades of journalism has taught me anything it's the value of punctuality. Turn up late, you miss the story. It's as simple as that.

A writer's study should be sacrosanct. It is where he makes his living. He needs the privacy to think. I close the door behind me. While I'm between jobs I intend to write a novel, the one I postponed after I met Julia. Decades ago.

Each day I wonder why it was me chosen for retrenchment. Each day I arrive at the same conclusion. I didn't fit into the new ethos. I unsettled other journalists. Okay, I'm loud and boisterous, rambunctious the Americans might call me, and opinionated, but that comes with confidence and experience, that came with knowing I was at the top of my game, that came with passion for my craft, that came with conviction. I was usually the first to arrive at the office, even before Dukakis most days. I was out on the streets, working, before most of them appeared. I had sources other than the internet. And when all the less dedicated staff had departed for the day, with excuses like it was their turn to pick up the kids or they had an urgent appointment, I returned to compile what I'd learned at the coalface, so to speak, while most of them, in reality, headed for a rowdy bar around the corner.

Don't get me wrong, I'm as fond of a drink as the next pressman, but the job comes—came—first. Which made it a vocation.

I believed Dukakis valued my effort. We always maintained a professional relationship, never allowing personal matters to intrude, although I'd heard from others that she had plenty to deal with. Our discussions were usually about the stories I was covering. Drug issues, homelessness, family violence, housing issues, although sometimes, when we digressed towards the current ominous technological developments threatening our livelihoods, the internet, social media, the twenty-four-hour news cycle, that kind of thing, our conversations became political. And here maybe I appeared too old fashioned, too plaintive. After all, she was my boss. She had some say in staffing matters.

As an editor who had experienced the historic barriers her gender faced in the workplace and had struggled all her working life to break through the glass ceiling, as they say, she was—is—fearless. She gave me the impression she'd like to see the entire political system turned on its head, with women running Canberra, perhaps for a decade, without a man in sight. I went along with the idea, just to humour her, even though I doubt it would make much difference. Look at Thatcher, whose greatest achievement was to win a war. She had bigger *cojones* than any of the tin-pot generals in the entire Argentine junta. Even our own Julia Gillard made little difference, although I enjoyed her *misogyny* speech, which was a gift to every journo in the country, the sort of speech I would've been proud of making myself, if I'd been a woman in politics. Then it crossed my mind Dukakis might have a similar plan for the newspaper. A daily broadsheet completely produced by women.

Not that she's a lesbian. According to rumours I've heard she has a penchant for young athletic men. I know she goes to the gym a lot. It annoys me she'd exclude some men, like me, on the basis of age, or physique. Mine isn't all that bad, although I think grey body hair, which I admit looks more singed than virile, doesn't help, the belly protrudes a tad too much, and the pectorals are soft and saggy, like most men my age. But isn't it the feminist criticism of men that they objectify women, judge them solely on their looks, with little or no regard for their intelligence or character? So, shouldn't a feminist like Dukakis adopt the same standards demanded of men? Anyway, what's the big deal about a six pack and buns? To me the contemporary ideal physique is fake. It looks like moulded plastic. I expected Dukakis to have more sophisticated taste with regard to the opposite sex. But I guess, like all of us, she's entitled to her contradictions.

Maybe I should write a book about that—*The Book of Contradictions*—ha, ha! Dukakis, Julia, just about everyone I know would have a chapter or two. And me, of course. I'm not that deluded or vain to think I don't have a few. But, if it's inclusive, it'd be a massive book, a thousand pages or more. I'm not sure I'm up for that at my age. Keep it to a couple of hundred pages. Maybe a romance is a better option. Something about an old journo on the cusp of retirement and an earnest young editor-in-chief. Write about what you know—that's the default advice given by most literary gurus. But there's got to be something in the mix that will keep the pages turning.

There's a raucous sound outside my window. The fucking wattlebird! Now on our flowering gum. I love the songs of most birds. Maggies. Cockies. Kookaburras. Even crows. Bellbirds. God, have you ever heard them? But I can't abide the wattlebird.

I know—I've mentioned this already.

I raise the blind and spot the culprit high up in the canopy. I release the brass sash-window lock and open the window, which makes its own uncooperative noise, put my head through, scraping my tonsured crown on the timber frame, breaking the skin and drawing blood, I'm sure, and with a fury I'm struggling to control, try to scare the nuisance away with hisses and aggressive grimaces and flailing hands.

Alas, this has no noticeable effect. The irritating creature stays put, out of reach, indifferent to the exertion below, which it has seen often enough in the past at this time of day.

I withdraw, rubbing my head tentatively with burgeoning self-pity, trying without a mirror to determine the damage, finding a smear of blood on my fingers, hardly a severed artery, shutting the window as quietly as possible, so as not to disturb Julia, still sleeping I suspect in the bedroom if this racket hasn't woken her.

My nerves are raw. And I'm not finished with the wattle-bird, which is one of our least colourful avian natives, a motley brown-grey with a dab of unprepossessing red on its neck, like a parsimonious concession to style, and a thin curved beak that reminds me of certain joyless people I've encountered over the years, some of them journalists, but usually working in finance somewhere, payroll or office budgets staff.

I pull the dressing gown around my expanding girth and put on a fez, which I feel accentuates my dignified mien, acquired on assignment in Egypt and hanging amongst the collection of headwear on the hat stand in our hallway. The boards creak with every step I take, suggesting the house needs restumping, another expense, or is it just my weight these days that animates the floor? I unlock the front door, step out onto the rotting timber porch, where the icy morning air snatches my breath away, extracts it in a column of pale vapour that soon dissipates, leaving no evidence it was a part of me. Clasping the dressing gown, I step onto the paving stones that run to the front gate and elsewhere. It's November but still the mornings are freezing. It rained all night. Everything is sodden. The trees still drip. I feel my scrotum crinkle and harden into a walnut shell, a rather unpleasant sensation.

Not far off the path, under the hedge that grows next to the fence, is a tap to which a hose is permanently connected. I take the trigger gun nozzle and turn the tap until the force builds, demanding a stronger grip. I walk towards the flowering gum with vindictive intent. Early this year despite the lingering wintry weather, it displays a vivid orange blossom, whose purpose no doubt is to attract pollinating creatures such as bees and wattlebirds but has the unfortunate side effect of intensifying the throbbing in my head. It's hard to believe Australian flora could be so dazzling.

Julia planted the tree a few years ago, a little too close to the house I thought at the time but said nothing since the garden, it had come to pass, was her domain, and she has done a good job of it, I have to admit. She has an excellent sense of horticultural *aesthetics*, if that's the right word for it, a pleasant balance of flower beds, bushes and trees.

The interior of the house, with the exception of my study, also reflects her conception of style: warm colours, tasteful Beardsley prints, although a tad out of fashion, even some original Aboriginal art on the walls, Persian rugs, soft furniture.

I can't fault it. But if I had my way, the place, inside and out, would look different. The flowering gum wouldn't have been so close to the house, where its roots are now lifting the pathing stones I laid to the unused bird bath near the side fence, at her request, a lot of my painstaking work getting ruined. I preferred a crimson blossom. She consulted with me but decided on the orange.

To be fair, I've never given domestic ambience much thought. As a writer, my mind has always been on the bigger picture, the world beyond the garden fence.

Approaching the tree surreptitiously this early in the morning, I squint. The colour is garish and the bloom so dense I can't see the wattlebird. I creep closer, the hose ready, my hand on the water gun trigger. I've done this before. Many times when birds or cats have annoyed me. I got the idea from the TV news. Discontent citizens on the street facing an authoritarian state's water cannons, the defiant ones swept off their feet when the riot police hit their target.

I fart. My first for the day that I am aware of. A loud one. A blokey one. And satisfying. But it has an unfortunate repercussion.

Hey, Gaddafi, what are you up to?

I hadn't noticed the neighbour in his front yard. He's moved out of my dream, where he was hoping to offer my wife his withered manhood, and is collecting his newspaper, the

News Limited thing I'd hazard a guess, bound in cling wrap, tossed into the yard from the local newsagent's car around 6.30am, usually doing minor damage to his garden, and now tucked under his arm. He smokes a cigarette, a stupid habit for a retired doctor to have, I would have thought. But there you go, another chapter for *Contradictions*. The well-educated are not always endowed with common sense, from my experience. I've reported on cases where judges try to lie about their identity when they're caught speeding, multi-millionaires are caught shop-lifting, and politicians fall into obvious traps that are set up to discredit them, knowing how their lust for power has blinded them, stupid things like that. They're manna to our profession. I admit I occasionally have a smoke, one or two a week, sometimes more when events are working in my favour, or going awry, but it's not an addiction. No danger in that.

The way he's standing, legs apart, facing me, suggests he's been watching me stalk the wattlebird. The Gaddafi reference baffles me, until I remember photos of the Libyan dictator in a fez. *Wrong country*, I retort.

He ignores me. *Eating plenty of roughage these days, are we?*

Breaking wind is a natural occurrence for every man, woman and child on Earth. Nuns and starlets and old Queen Elizabeth. Jesus, the Virgin Mary and Mohammed must have farted too. And the doctor. So why the snide comment? He'd know the statistics, surely? I recently read it occurs on average fourteen times a day, a figure that leaves me feeling slightly anxious and abnormal, and has me counting, although before midday it has slipped my mind, wilfully or because my profession has taught me to question statistical methodology, or other matters have superseded it, I cannot say.

After the disparaging remark, the doctor hardly pauses before he declares, *It's a bit superfluous, watering the garden, don't you think? It came down in buckets last night or haven't you noticed?*

I look at him, look at the hose, and shrug. It's too early in the morning for a riposte. Without a throbbing head, I'd try, but not today. Then I remember something about him. *Ready to sign our petition, Doc?* I call. It's Julia's petition, really, in support of a permit to build a homeless refuge in our neighbourhood, a counter petition to the one he's organised opposing a hostel or any other social service that might impact on local property values.

You've got to be joking. Contempt modulates his laughter. *You're nuts.*

Worried about your assets, are you, Doc? Isn't there something in your hypocritical oath, or whatever the bloody thing's called, about showing a bit of humanity?

He rises on his toes as if to deliver his next statement from a greater height. *I don't need to learn humanity from a communist!*

He's formed an opinion about my politics from the few disagreeable conversations we've had and the posters Julia has placed in one of our front windows, supporting campaigns to improve public transport, to increase housing for the poor and the homeless, and to ban coal-fired power plants. He's also seen me in a Che Guevara T-shirt, mistaking my only concession to fashion for a political pronouncement.

I don't disabuse him. Instead I burst into the chorus of *The Internationale*, which I learned while covering the MUA-Patricks dispute on the wharves years ago, and, again resorting to the TV, copying an ad this time, for what I can't remember, I swing the hose towards him, pull the trigger, and watch his jaw drop and his eyes close as he tries to comprehend what's happening.

The impact breaks his vainglorious stance, forces him back a little, although not to the same degree as a water cannon would, regrettably. Water drips from the end of his nose. His soaked skivvy, for he has no jumper or jacket on despite the chill, clings to his concave chest, a wet fag dangling from his lips. Lucky the paper is still in its plastic wrap.

What the fuck! he cries.

You're lucky I'm not Gaddafi, you quack, and I brandish the hose like a pistol just as I've seen Gaddafi do on TV, *or this thing might be lethal.* There! The riposte! That makes me feel a whole lot better.

I return to the tap, turn it off, toss the hose aside and head indoors, glancing at him as he shouts something, causing a dog somewhere to start barking, an unusual disturbance in our neighbourhood, especially early weekend mornings.

Inside, when the door is closed, I high-five a phantom and utter *Yes!* although I make sure it is barely audible so as not to disturb Julia. I'm always mindful of her despite how tepid our relationship seems to have become in recent times.

I creep back into my study. I want to write but the interruption has dispersed my thoughts. Besides, my head is still throbbing. I sit and stare at the screen. I don't really want to reminisce about last night's dinner party where I upset Julia and probably ruined any chance of intimacy soon, although there's a novel in that, surely? My dream comes back to me. Part erotic. Part mockery. Alas, these days even my dreams are desolate, and there, too, lies the makings of a good novel.

A colleague once told me that regular ejaculation of semen was critical for the health of the prostate or otherwise it would stagnate like a billabong inside the innocuous little organ. He was trying to justify the spate of affairs he was having and suggested I follow his example. For a few years now my prostate has been giving me some problems. Not that it's cancerous, a common enough fate for a man of my age. My PSA test shows only a borderline risk and I've been digitally examined by a urologist, which has revealed a large but regular shaped prostate—nothing to be worried about. It gives some discomfort, putting pressure on my bladder as it fills during the night, and forces me out of bed two or three times while Julia sleeps. I try to avoid disturbing her, but I know it does when, in the mornings, she grumbles about my *nocturnal meanderings*, as she calls my unavoidable trips to and from the ensuite.

She doesn't realise I lie awake, trying not to move, hoping the sensation will pass, losing precious sleep, trying to avoid disturbing her, until pressure builds like flood waters against a dam wall. Then I slip out of bed. The alternative doesn't bear thinking about. Sometimes, especially when I flush, she stirs enough to complain, to threaten separate rooms. That is the last thing I want.

But what can I do to prevent that pool of semen stagnating? I close the study door, re-adjust the height of the chair, and turn to the computer.

I don't suppose it would surprise anyone if I were to admit that I seriously considered my colleague's advice. But I've stumbled upon a simpler solution. It's not the thing a self-respecting pressman would contemplate. He'd be at a bar, chatting to a solitary woman, intriguing her with irresistible anecdotes from the job. But my days of casual sex are over, not that I fear rejections, it's more a matter of maintaining some dignity, at least in the eyes of others.

I open my search engine. The home page is set on Google. I click on *Images*. I hesitate. Again a matter of dignity. I don't type the obvious. I have an acute inquisitive mind, necessary in my line of work. And I like to think each time I enter the virtual world I'm open to learning something new. I don't subscribe to the saying *you can't teach an old dog new tricks*. I type in *tantric sex*.

The parental control is off. We don't need it. We have no children, although not for want of trying. I've had my sperm count tested and I have to say the problem doesn't lie with me.

Many photos of naked couples in various gymnastic coital poses appear on the screen, plus other images of ancient Indian erotic relief sculptures, and some diagrams depicting bodily pleasure points, which are neglected apparently in conventional love making but are all the go in tantric. I click on *Video.*

The one that attracts my attention is titled *Tantric Sex with Ebony Goddess.* The designation should have warned me it was a ruse that had little to do with the revered Hindu practice and much to do with plain, old, sordid porn. All the ebony goddess is wearing is a band of filigree gold around her waist. The man is soon out of his suit, his quivering erection twice the size my own. I watch them for a while, performing erotic contortions, but nothing Julia and I haven't tried, although, admittedly, not for a very long time and not as accomplished as this. *God, that's hardly possible!* I mutter.

What are you doing? It's an incredulous, reproachful voice. Julia has entered the room.

An unpleasant tsunami of adrenalin crashes into my brain.

Bloody hell, Frank, I didn't know you had sunk so low!

How did I not notice her approach? How did I not hear the door open? Usually it makes a bit of noise. The hinges need oiling but I prefer them squeaky for just such an occasion. Maybe she oiled them, intending and planning this trap. Was I so engrossed I failed to feel her presence? Or am I just going deaf? Something else to worry about. Once before when Julia accused me of not listening to her, I thought I might be going deaf. She wouldn't accept the possibility, told me to get the wax removed.

What are you doing, creeping up on me like that? I yell, literally yell, in an attempt to return some of the guilt that surfed in on the tsunami, with all the histrionics of an amateur thespian. *You scared the living daylights out of me.*

She's shaking her head, her auburn hair afire. *I heard someone shouting outside. It woke me up. Then I heard you coming back inside. What's going on? After last night, can't we have a bit of peace and quiet? It's Saturday morning for God's sake! What have you got that ridiculous fez on for? And what are you doing perving at pornography? Really, Frank, I can hardly believe you'd do this.*

I shrug, far too late to minimise the video, but I click the *pause* icon, which captures the couple doing some kind of conjoined cartwheel. *It was that cranky old bugger next door. What's he call himself? Stanley Herbert-Jones? Oh, sorry,* Doctor *Stanley Herbert-Jones. The name says it all, if you ask me. I demanded he sign your petition. He refused. So I turned the hose on him.*

Julia gapes at me. *You what?*

I turned the hose on him. Just like in that corny ad you used to laugh at every time it came on. Don't deny it. You laughed! I gave him a bloody good soaking.

Now she is laughing, but it's not mirthful laughter. It's *I'm married to a madman* laughter, which is unfair, since we've never really married, although we've talked about it now and then, and almost always refer to each other as *husband* and *wife*, but it has just always seemed like an expense we could do without. *And that's the way to change his mind, is it?*

Good point, I think, but don't articulate.

And this? She points at the computer.

I adopt a defiant expression. *What do you think it is?*

I switch to my hurt mien, but she's unmoved. *It's porn, Frank, disgusting porn. And sitting there in that ridiculous fez makes you look all the more depraved, don't ask me why.*

I have an out-of-body experience, see myself from above. It's a corpulent degenerate I'm looking at, who repulses me but also arouses my deepest pity—*Jesus,* I mutter.

Her indignation is magnificent. She's radiant. She has already cleaned up the messy mascara and combed her hair, I notice. And she doesn't appear to be hungover. Maybe she didn't drink as much as me. Always the perfect host(ess). It's a long time since I've seen her looking so vibrant, so young. Astonishing, if you factor in last night's—entertainment—for want of a better word.

She's in her early fifties, although her exact age and date of birth momentarily eludes me, some time in December. Being a pessimist, I'm wilfully oblivious to everyone's birthdays. The countdown I call it. But she's precious about it. It's the twentieth, I think, but I better check before the day arrives or our relationship will erode further.

Relationship is a terrible, imprecise word—*marriage* is closer but has limitations. With all the myriad words in the English language, where is the one that comes close to defining two people who have shared their lives intimately without official sanction? *De facto* is a poor substitute and is merely an adjective. But I recall someone asking of Julia and me if we were an *item*. Maybe *item* is the word I'm looking for.

Despite her aura of youth this morning, her red hair has strands of grey. It lends her an air of dignity and wisdom, which I'm not convinced she deserves. Not that she's stupid. Far from it. She recently completed a PhD, which has been published as a hardback. Very impressive. But at times what I think is blindingly obvious can genuinely baffle her. Sometimes I suspect she actually gets it but is being ironic to humour herself at my expense. Yet normally she puts such a literal interpretation on circumstances whose understanding requires some degree of subtlety or ambiguity, like when her boss—her head of faculty, *team leader* she likes to call him, whatever—when he asked her to accompany him to a conference in Bali, she thought his intentions were honourable or professional or some such nonsense. Couldn't she read between the lines? Doesn't she understand anything? He wanted her to operate his PowerPoint while he delivered his research findings, or rather the findings of his underlings, which he was happy to put his name to. Interesting how a two-day conference turned into a week. Why waste a good trip to Bali?

Of course, I love her (whatever that means in this day and age). I appreciate her sense of humour. It usually takes a few wines before she hits her stride but then she can be hilarious. And I still like her body despite a few sags and droops here and there. When I get the chance to see her naked these days I think of Rubens or Matisse rather than Schiele. But the intensity of emotion? Where has that gone?

Frank? Are you listening?

I glance at her. Suddenly I feel a tremendous sadness, a terrible grief, for what we're losing. *What do you think I'm doing?* I say, still wanting to sound hurt. *It's research. Dukakis seemed interested in a series of articles on contemporary youth when I suggested it.*

Julia finds it hard to see a connection between topic and source material, one hand upon her ample hip, the other gesticulating. *Have you forgotten she sacked you?*

I nod and emit an exasperated sigh. *It's called redundancy, my love, my wildflower of the campus—I mean the pampas. I'm afraid a stellar career, an inviolable reputation, wasn't enough to protect me from the tyranny of technological change. But there's still freelance opportunities. Dukakis promised she'd look at it. I think she's already regretting letting me go. Within a week or two she would've realised what a mistake she made. Interesting to check how the sales figures are trending. But if she wants me to continue I'll be gracious enough to oblige. I'm above vindictiveness, even if it is at the expense of my novel, which is now what I really want to focus on, and is well underway, if you were wondering. No? Not wondering? Anyway, why shy away from adolescent sexual mores? Fearlessness and curiosity are the hallmarks of great journalism.* I wave at the screen and express my disgust with a clever manoeuvre of my lips and tongue, with my hand discreetly detouring past my head to remove the fez, which I drop to the floor.

She sighs. *Yes, yes, but what's porn got to do with youth culture?*

Julia! What universe are you living in?

Not this one, I hope. She gestures at the screen.

I'm smitten with disappointment. *Well, as a journalist, it's incumbent upon me to cover all angles.*

She slants her head awry for a better look. *They're certainly at odd angles.*

Are they? I haven't paid it much attention. My hypocrisy is palpable. *Apparently watching interracial sex is trending for under 25s. Unbelievable.*

She peers at the screen again. Her eyes are wide. Desultory laughter punctuates her uneasiness. She steers the conversation elsewhere. *Dukakis is duping you, Frank. Throwing you a few crumbs, to make you think she cares, trying to get everyone to believe that your fate was out of her control. But it's bullshit. She made you redundant, while she retained others less worthy of the job. Where's your pride? You're a good journalist, Frank, you were great in your day. Don't let the changes that are coming defeat you. The Frank I thought I lived with would start looking for another job. There must be half a dozen digital newspapers that'd take you on at the drop of a hat.*

Glancing down at the fez I grunt at her allusion to my humiliation, but it's an odd sound. *Sweetheart, redundancy's a blessing in disguise. This is the chance I've been waiting for, to write that book I've been talking about for years—*

Decades.

Decades then. You know that's what I've wanted but my job has always come first. Well, not anymore. I'm looking at this as an opportunity. I'm a glass half full man.

She snorts derisively. I try to stay calm. She has never taken my literary aspirations seriously. *All I want from you, Julia, sweetheart, is your blessing.*

It goes without saying. But if you're so keen to write a book, why bother pandering to Dukakis? You're not feeling insecure, are you, Frank? You used to be such a fighter. If you want to write a novel, go for it. Show some passion. Even if you get nowhere, I'd still admire you more than the dithering old fuddy duddy you're becoming. She comes close, puts an arm around my shoulder and peers at the screen. The castigation is over and her irrepressible buoyant mood returns. *God, that's so gynaeco-logical,* she says. *Does it turn you on?*

I shrug. *Vaguely, but you're missing the point. Maybe this's what the young people enjoy and I'm trying to understand Gen X and Y. Is there a Z yet? It's bloody hard to keep up these days. There must be a Z by now.*

They're called Millennials.

I nod, only half-listening. *Even kids look at this and their parents don't seem to care.*

Julia rubs my pate affectionately, a sign she's fallen for my argument. Relieved, I use the opportunity to close Google.

You'd be better off approaching young people and asking them if they watch this stuff rather than watching it yourself. That's not going to tell you what they think of it, is it?

Don't you think I've thought of that? I say sharply, feeling out-manoeuvred. *But can you imagine how they'd react to a stranger asking them questions about pornography?*

She looks at me queerly for a moment. *They might think you're an old perv.*

Exactly!

She sighs. *We never needed this stuff when we were their age, did we?*

I glance at her. I notice her eyes are blue. If someone had asked me about their colour yesterday I would have hesitated, unsure. You can live with someone for years, decades, and still take little notice of certain things about them.

She massages my shoulders. *We used to think we were so sophisticated,* she says, *but, my God, we were babes in the woods compared to today's lot.*

She squeezes hard, presses her thumbs into the tender area between my shoulder blades. The pain is acute. Unexpected. It forces a howl from me. *Woaaah!*

She chuckles and gives my shoulders a matronly pat. *You are so tight across here, old boy. Feels like years of tension. What have you got to be tense about?* She raises her eyebrows, a sign of levity, or facetiousness, as if she's privy to all my secrets. *Why don't you get a proper massage? There's plenty of masseuses around these days. There's one at our local shopping centre. I've been there. It's Thai. You'll love it.*

She senses my resistance to her suggestion. *Spend a bit of money on yourself, Frank. Why be a Spartan? Why wear a hair-shirt all your life? Some people indulge themselves every week. Once in a while won't hurt you, you know.*

I ignore the mixed metaphor. A Spartan in a hair-shirt doesn't work for me. Those warriors with their oiled pectorals and loose leather loin cloths weren't exactly into mortification of the flesh. *How quickly you forget my earning capacity is temporarily challenged.*

She pats my shoulders. *What about this best seller you're intending to write? Aren't you expecting a million-dollar advance?* Chuckling, she bends, gives me a peck on the cheek and heads for the door. *Don't forget to put plenty of sex in it, my boy, or it won't sell. Maybe you can borrow some of those scenes.* She gestures vaguely at the computer as she leaves. *In the meantime, I'll give you some money,* she calls from the passage.

Sex scenes? Excellent suggestion, but I can hardly rely on our recent history, can I? I sit in the wake of her indulgence. Silence washes over me. My mind is struggling with her largesse. She has always considered me niggardly. I just don't waste money on things I don't need. Unlike her, I'm not an impulsive buyer. I'm cautious with money, that's all. I respect it. One of the reasons I was given more than one stint as an overseas correspondent was my prudence with the newspaper's money. But this has been a sore point between Julia and me. She interprets my parsimonious proclivity as a criticism of her spending habits. So her guilt becomes an accusation. *I live with a tight-arse,* I overheard her say one day, in a jocular tone, which maddened me because it sounded patronising, like it was a minor blemish she was prepared to endure, or she was aware of my defects but was endowed with enough generosity of spirit to overlook them, turning my shortcomings into her virtues. Mostly she won't hear a bad word said about me, and before her friends she is fulsome in her praise, which I suspect is so that they have scant grounds for criticising her choice. Not that I lose sleep over their opinions of me. Not often, anyway.

I sit at the computer once more, open Google, click on Images.

The door is open again and Julia returns. I snap off Google.

By the way, she says, *happy birthday.*

My head swivels. I frown at her and feign, *It's not my birthday, is it?*

She rolls her eyes. *It's the fourteenth, Frank. Why else were you talking so much about Charlie last night?*

Was I? I frown again in an attempt to convey vague recollection.

God, you really don't remember? Her eyes widen in disbelief.

Poor old Charlie. Has it been a year already? Disinclined to talk more about him, perhaps because I said too much last night,

I turn back to the computer to check its date, which is credible since I no longer have a job or any other reason to remember dates. I point at the screen. *Fourteenth! You're right.* I offer her another puzzled expression. *I haven't heard from my sisters yet.*

Strange how neither of them has rung. I never expect a call from my brother, who only rings when he wants me to do something for him or one of my articles enrages him. But my sisters never forget. They always ring first thing in the morning. To get it over with. Like going to vote early. Duty done, no matter how tedious, then they can relax for the rest of the day. Perhaps they are sick of hearing me pretend I've forgotten my own birthday. Perhaps they're tired of listening to me say I'd rather they didn't remind me. Perhaps they finally feel aggrieved because, like my brother, I never ring them with birthday wishes or send a card, which these days cost a fortune unless they're those hideously stupid-humoured things that fill almost an entire aisle at a supermarket. If I sent one of these they would judge me harshly. And we're all well past sending presents.

Maybe they've finally got the message, Julia suggests. *I have.*

So, my birthday. Only this perfunctory felicitation from Julia, and nothing, not a word from my siblings or the few people I still call friends, which is unexpectedly depressing, as if I mean little to anyone anymore, if I ever have. Partly my fault, since I've hidden the date on my Facebook page. Maybe it's just too early in the morning. I won't criticise anyone yet. I'll give them until midday.

Come and have some breakfast with me for a change, she says and heads for the kitchen, another surprise because I thought we always had breakfast together. At the very least we sit at the same table, at the same time.

But then it dawns on me she means we should share break-fast and perhaps converse, which is not what usually happens because I listen to the radio news, using headphones, while I eat. Julia can't bear the world intruding so early in the day, whereas I have to know what's happening. As I used to say to her, *I need to know if the world still exists before I go to work, no point otherwise.*

I hear the wattlebird again and consider returning to the garden to accomplish what I failed to do on my earlier foray, until I realise I don't have the energy for it.

■

Feeling defeated, and not just by a wattle-bird but by the burden of each moment, I follow Julia to the kitchen, where she's already making pikelets from a pre-mixture she must have bought at the supermarket, since she's pouring it directly into the pan from a plastic container, a convenient but on a couple of levels—culinary and commitment-wise—not altogether satisfactory accomplishment. Besides, I was expecting my usual—bacon and eggs.

As always on a Saturday she is in her bathrobe. While she labours quietly at the stove with her back to me, I'm overcome by the feeling she's lonely, but this is possibly misplaced, a projection. While I look at her back, her rounded shoulders and sensuous rump, a wave of affection overcomes me from which I'm struggling to surface, gasping for air. How did she end up with me? An appalling choice. I'm not so deluded that I can't see that. She could have made any number of men her partner but she accepted my offer, or rather my presence, I suspect out of pity, which she mistook for love. And now loneliness and regret. I see it sculpted into her posture, etched into her face, and presented to me as readymade pikelets. She gives me an affectionate peck on the cheek. I'm grateful she's decided not to berate me for my conduct last night, or at least to postpone any rebuke until my birthday's over.

I put my hand under her bathrobe, touch her thigh, fleetingly, fleetingly. As if it horrifies her, she moves away, back to the stove to pour more of the ready-mix solution. The sensation of soft flesh lingers on my fingertips. I long for her. I long to touch her. But these days there's a mysterious barrier.

I don't understand what it is or how it got there. An indeterminate force as potent as gravity. Neither of us can ignore it but endeavour to wrap our apprehension in silence.

The pikelets are edible only after I add honey. They stick to my palate but I make no complaint. I'm grateful for her effort, considering her culinary indifference and inconsistencies in the quality of the meals she presents me. But I'm no master chef, myself, so I make a fulsome noise while I use my tongue to dislodge each piece from the roof of my mouth and chew, express my approval, for effort rather than quality, express my gratitude, for her loyalty, her still being here, her still being prepared to put aside her despair to cook for me on my birthday.

Just eat, Frank, she says, *and don't make a fool of yourself.*

I look around in surprise. *But there's no one else here,* I say.

The spatula goes into overdrive on the hotplate. *I'm here,* she sighs emphatically, and her free hand draws some hair behind an ear. A wistful gesture, I think. She wants to be anywhere but here.

What are your plans for—the day? I ask but am tempted to say *the rest of your life.*

She slips onto the chair opposite me at the table with her own plate of pikelets. Her eyes are steady, observing me, with pity I suspect, with obsolete love and grief for her life of daily disappointments, each so minor and transient it is hardly worth mentioning, like one dot on a pointillist painting, or, to put it more contemporaneously, one pixel. But step back and observe the entire picture and it's easy to see it resembles me.

There is golden syrup in a squirt bottle, which she applies to her bland repast with unnecessary force, bottle upside down, both hands around it in a strangler's grip.

This year I've taken you at your word, she says. *So I haven't arranged any celebrations. No surprise party. No restaurant booking. No weekend escape. No cake. No present. Instead I'll leave you alone. I'm spending the day with a friend and later I'll stay at Mum's the night. Consider my offer to pay for a massage a present, if you like. And that's the last you'll hear of your birthday from me, in accordance with your wishes, Frank.*

I nod. But I'm almost overwhelmed by a feeling of betrayal. A feeling of worthlessness. Of redundancy. Fifty-five. Fucking hell, how quickly it's gone! It seems like yesterday I was twenty. But it's thirty-five years ago. Another thirty-five—tomorrow—and I'll be in the grave. Gone forever. Nothing left. Hardly anything left already.

What are you looking so glum about? she says with genuine concern. *I thought this is what you wanted.*

I switch my gaze from the coffee cup to her face and see a stranger. The woman I've lived with for the past twenty or so years is a different person somehow. I notice things I've never seen before: a small scar at the corner of her mouth, a blemish on her cheek, a puffiness under her chin, a harshness in her face she is unable to conceal. Suddenly I realise that she is not an extension of me. She's a person in her own right. An epiphany that flummoxes me.

Have I always considered her an extension of my self? Maybe but I doubt it. There must have been a time, early on at least, when she was an entity in her own right or I would never have noticed her, surely? At what point did she become just a part of my routine?

I remember when we first met how she struck me as unique. That's what caught my attention. She was haughty. And haughtiness suggested nobody's minion.

It was at Melbourne University on the path outside the Baillieu Library at the start of my honours year when I first noticed her. I was sitting on the grass with a small, chummy group of undergraduates, all of them male, discussing, if I remember rightly, James Joyce and the significance to literature of *Ulysses,* with Craig L Codrington-Smith (another of those hyphenated bores), offering us his latest insights into the origins of *stream of consciousness* as a literary device. I was hardly paying attention. My eyes were fixed on Julia, obviously a fresher, who had some books under one arm and was struggling to find something in her shoulder bag, the hem of her summer dress rippling in a breeze.

She was stunning. Absolutely beautiful. Auburn, shoulder-length hair, slender neck, and sensual mouth that pouted in mild frustration as the object of her search eluded her.

I was mesmerized.

How I remember what we were discussing is due to the manner in which Codrington-Smith's own stream of consciousness veered seamlessly into an invitation for Julia to join our little group. She abandoned her search, looked across at him, lowered her sunglasses on her nose and raised an eyebrow. *And why would I want to join an intellectual wanker like you?* she retorted with implied familiarity. *You and your hero,* pointing at a copy of *Ulysses* on the lawn, *are both pathetic fantasists.* Then with her head titled sideways both eyebrows challenged him to deny it before she turned and strode into the library.

Remarkable for a fresher—I remember thinking.

I pursued her for months before even speaking to her, put myself in her path at every opportunity, endeavouring to get her to notice me without appearing to be aware of her. I followed her home discreetly, tried to discover her habits, her interests.

How many times I sat in the seat behind her at the Carlton Moviehouse I can't recall. The good thing was she often went alone without a companion, male or female, which suggested she had a serious interest in the cinematic arts, about which I knew nothing, short of a few Hollywood names. I had to force myself to watch the movies rather than the back of her head, preparing for the moment when our first encounter eventuated. I wanted her to know we had something in common. We had seen the same movies, appreciated the same art form.

To this end I read every cinematic magazine, every movie review, every Hollywood history and gossip omnibus I could get my hands on, neglecting my academic studies, with the exception of critical theory and my analysis of the sexist assumptions to be found in *Ulysses*.

One day she sat next to me at the movies. It was no accident. Once I realised that she sat in the same aisle, same seat whenever possible, I simply arrived early. Despite the cinema being half empty, she sat next me, almost defiantly, as if I'd encroached on her territory.

I was afraid she could hear my heart pounding.

In a serendipitous moment I was able to mutter to myself, *Oh God, this movie is so sexist,* and felt her gaze shift fleetingly from the screen to me, which was enough to prompt a comment when the lights came on and the credits were rolling that my utterance was fairly enlightened for a guy.

I can't remember the movie but it led to a discussion of sexism in cinema and the arts in general in which I acquitted myself quite well apparently because the next thing we're having coffee and the next thing we're in her bed fucking like a couple of frenzied devotees of Eros.

Afterwards she confessed that she had been aware of my presence for a number of weeks and had deliberately sat next to me, hoping she might get a chance to speak to someone who shared her commitment to cinema. She had even noticed me on campus and had been tempted to approach me there, where I'd been careful to keep my distance from the *pathetic fantasist* Craig L Codrington-Smith, with whom it transpires she probably had more in common, since he went on to become a professor of literature, or some such thing, in the United States, until his career was cut short by a disgruntled student with a handgun.

I've never revealed my role in our chance encounter and was astonished by its success. She was such a strong character in those days, such a separate entity, so intimidating with her beauty and intellect that it is difficult to imagine how we arrived at a point where I would take her for granted. But it happened. She developed a dual entity—one the extension of me and the other this stranger, whom I'm looking at now, who has co-existed all these years in the same house but has lived an entirely autonomous existence.

No, I'm not really glum. Well, maybe a little. I almost mention Charlie but think better of it. *It's just that now you've done this for me I feel so selfish. I realise what a selfish bugger I've been all these years.* And I sigh profoundly to highlight my anguish.

She moves closer to comfort me. *We're all selfish,* she says philosophically. *Okay, there are times when I do feel you're inconsiderate, but I'm not going to get into an argument about how selfish you can be. I'll just get out of your hair for the day, metaphorically speaking.* Her vision and a patronising hand alight on my balding dome.

I attempt a grateful smile which unfortunately takes the form of a grimace. *Who's the friend you're meeting?* I ask and she looks away evasively, out the glass wall at the rear of the house, which opens onto our garden where the plants she loves grow.

Oh, just a uni friend. You wouldn't enjoy it.

Wouldn't enjoy what? It sounds like a subterfuge. Jealousy, regret, apprehension are tiny daggers gathering around my heart, hurtful pricks but not yet piercing it.

She feels the need to elaborate. *We may have a coffee, but I'm helping with their thesis. Technical stuff. Nothing interesting.*

And of course I am interested now, but not from any academic angle. It's the possessive adjective. *Their* not *his* or *her*. That would reveal too much. My guess is *his*. With my head pushing forward, I frown, somewhat more affected and supercilious than previous frowns. *That young nerd you invited here last night? What's his name?*

At her dinner party, which I've been morosely trying to forget, held on the eve of my birthday, probably as a way of expressing her contempt for my reluctance to celebrate it—*if your birthday's not important to you, Frank, I'm sure you won't mind me having a dinner party instead*—and, worse, held on the first anniversary of the death of Charlie—at her dinner party there was a gormless, introspective type whose sole contribution to the conversation was to give a Marxist perspective on Islamic terrorism.

Peter? Oh, yeah, I forgot he was here, she says, shrugging, realising her vagueness sounds like deceit. *He's such an unobtrusive guy. Just discovered Marx, apparently.*

I harrumph. *It's a pity Comrade Charlie's not around anymore. He'd be over the moon to know the universities are still producing Marxists.* Immediately I kick myself for mentioning Charlie again. Enough damage was done at the dinner party.

You already made that point last night, remember?

I put my earplugs in and turn the radio on, hoping she won't pursue the opportunity I've created.

The news is all bad. Worse than bad. Horrific. Over a hundred civilians have been slaughtered in France. *Jesus, listen to this!* I stammer.

I extract the earplugs from the radio so Julia can hear. She pushes aside the last of her pikelets and we sit in silence for ten minutes, occasionally exchanging glances, drawn close again by an atrocity.

God, just last night we were discussing the probability of something like this happening. What's the world coming to? she laments. *Who are these evil little men? Surely Islam doesn't condone such atrocities?*

I make a futile gesture. *Charlie would say George Bush, not Islam, is to blame for all this,* I reply, *by destabilising the entire Middle East, creating a vacuum that these fanatics would gladly fill, spreading this scourge across the world like a cancer.*

Julia rises, furious at me, at the world, at her pleasant day spoiled.

Oh, for God's sake, Frank, this is not the time for political analysis. It's a moral outrage. Nothing justifies it. Not American stupidity. Not cultural humiliation. Nothing.

I throw up my arms in a defensive gesture. *I'm just predicting what Charlie would say.*

She takes her plate to the sink, disposes of it demonstrably, and leaves the kitchen.

I turn the radio off. The kitchen is a mess. Plates from dinner last night are piled up on the bench. Their smell is almost overpowering. All those exotic Thai curry odours that linger mercilessly. Neither of us has bothered to load the dishwasher.

It's my birthday, the one day when it's accepted a person is released from the daily grind of household chores, about which, anyway, with regard to the dishwasher, we're in a kind of Mexican standoff because somehow with the passage of time Julia has come to regard it as my responsibility, just like the rubbish bins, or when a loose bracket or hinge needs tightening, or a tap washer or light bulb replaced.

Admittedly she usually washes our bed linen and towels, and she cooks more often than I do, which is a good thing, given the extent and standard of my culinary repertoire.

Last night she cooked. We had guests. Her guests. This Peter fellow and a few of her work colleagues, including her boss (apologies, team leader). I never cook when we have guests.

I'm not allowed to cook for her guests. I'd be expected to cook if they were my guests. I never have guests.

I endure these dinners she arranges. Four a year is the routine, with the odd extra dinner for special occasions, which allows her to entertain the whole gamut of friends, people of influence amongst them, on average six a dinner, so around thirty annually, which personally I feel is too many.

Nourishing her community, she claims. Does she know how much it costs?

Personally I can't accept they're all friends. I have four. Friends not dinners. I had five until Charlie died of cancer, a loss of twenty percent of my inner circle. Most good journos don't have many friends, they have contacts, of which there can be hundreds. Nor do I call colleagues friends, although Julia makes no such distinction. I never called Dukakis a friend, although there was one time when we came close to crossing the line.

Even then, *friendship* is not really the right word. I'll try to explain. The feelings I had for her, since the very first day she entered our office, when that electricity of attraction passed between us the moment our eyes met, were just a wild animal reaction with the potential to ruin my contented and comfortable existence. I knew that if anything happened between us, it would be intense. It could never be a *casual* affair, separated from the rest of my life. At times difficult to subdue, I was able to deal with the daily distraction of Chloe Dukakis in my own private way, until one day when she arrived at work shortly after me, before the rest of our colleagues appeared, and my defences were almost shattered. Usually intense, sometimes manic, there's nothing like an empty newspaper office for atmosphere and foreboding. She sat at her desk and burst into tears.

I had an inkling of what this was about. I occasionally over-heard her talking to others about the parlous state of her marriage. But here, with just the two of us alone in the office, I suffered the terrifying thought that she was about to declare her feelings for me.

Oh, Munro, I don't know what to do, she said, elbows on a desk, hands shielding her eyes.

It was the moment when I could have approached and put my hands on her shoulders, the moment when the life I'd been leading for the last fifteen years would have come to an abrupt end. I panicked. I admit to my share of casual affairs, which were always brief, as brief as the act itself on some occasions, and never involving colleagues or any sort of commitment, for, witnessing it in others at the office, I learnt that those affairs were too fraught and risky.

Despite my desire to have sex with Chloe Dukakis it never crossed my mind that I would ever leave Julia. My hopes were always that Chloe might approach me after work and whisper she wanted a few hours of fornication, no strings attached, and nobody need find out. Of course this was just a puerile fantasy and I knew it. As her sobbing became more pronounced and I became more alarmed, I suggested she make an appointment with our workplace counsellor. She glanced wistfully across at me and nodded and pulled herself together.

It was the closest we ever came to intimacy of any sort, excluding the occasional kiss on the cheek at the start of a new year, or the end of an old one, or a birthday, or some other office-calendar occasion.

By the time our colleagues showed up both of us were engrossed in paperwork. There was no evidence of the existential crisis that had just occurred. After that we moved inexorably into a carefully nuanced professional relationship, although I suspect the lapse was behind her decision to select me for redundancy. It's a tad ironic, I'd say, that she began to criticise my writing for its sentimentality. *You're romanticising the past too much, Munro,* she said one day, shortly before she announced my departure. *You've got to move into the twenty-first century. Your articles are being ignored.* Me, sentimental? I was a hard-hitting journalist. There was no pulling punches. I never sugar-coated anything. Me, *sentimental?* I took umbrage at the suggestion.

Julia has never gotten wind of any of my wayward thoughts or any of the brief affairs I've had, thank God, or she too might have used them as an excuse to ditch me.

There are times when I feel that's what she's looking for.

Julia's relationship to *her* colleagues is far less clearly defined.

At her dinner party last night I noticed the rapport she has established with her immediate boss—sorry, team leader—an associate professor of political science, a George somebody—I'm bad with names—an earnest intellectual accustomed to being the fulcrum of discourse, at least amongst the group of academic diners that Julia had assembled. (I can only imagine what happened between them in Bali. I have no evidence.) His molluscan lips were moistened constantly with the best from our cellar, his jaded eyes coming to rest time and again on Julia's cleavage, which moved like dough rising in a warm place, although probably indiscernible to all but me and George.

For a while I was barely noticed amongst these luminaries, who offered post-modern interpretations of the post-9/11 crises and the resurgence of international terrorism, which held Julia in thrall, until I, as a journalist with international experience, made my contribution. Perhaps they thought what I had to say was irrelevant, as if my paucity of academic credentials should have rendered me mute. I would need a doctorate in journalism for her guests to have taken any notice. Admittedly, I did stray from the topic into personal matters once or twice.

I look around the kitchen and it strikes me that I'm mute here as well, symbolically speaking. There is nothing of mine to be seen. The kitchen has been arranged to suit Julia. She sees herself as head cook in this household.

The kitchen is white with charcoal coloured stone bench tops and low-hanging pendant lights, artfully placed jars of nuts and herbs, a spice rack, pots and pans hanging like ready-made sculptures, a large bowl of in-season fruit, an environmentalist calendar, elegant breakfast stools, just like you see in those interior design magazines. I can't question her taste. I repeat, she has a good aesthetic eye.

Of the other rooms in the house only my study and to a lesser extent the living room, where I have my own ageing leather armchair, turned-timber reading lamp with beige linen shade and a scalloped side table, show some sign of my cohabitation. I inherited the reading lamp from my father, who liked to read the articles I wrote for the *National Times* by it, early on in my career, so that we would have something to argue about. I picked up the side table, where I keep the latest books I'm reading, from the trash-or-treasure market that I visit with Julia occasionally, to keep the peace with her as she exercises her democratic right to shop.

Even the bedroom is predominately her space. She's spread her apparel through most of the walk-in robe, the chest of drawers and the ensuite, her bric-a-brac strategically placed like boundary markers around our rooms.

I use an old wardrobe in the spare room and tend to favour the bathroom near the laundry, which I guess you could say has my stamp upon it: my shaving gear and toothbrush, my bathrobe and spare slippers, a set of scales (whose accuracy is suspect) to keep an eye on my weight, which despite my best efforts has crept up over the years, and my obsolete shower cap, which Julia might use on the rare occasions she ventures into the shower downstairs.

It is a long time since we've showered together, longer still since we've had sex in that humid cubicle, which became so awkward we agreed we were getting too old (and oversized) for antics that might look erotic on the big (or little) screen but, like much that Hollywood offers, has little connection to (non-celluloid/non-digital) reality.

I admit I'd love to shower with her again, if just for the touch of her skin, her buttocks, her breasts and lower down, which was once a source of delight and wonder, with soft water pouring over all parts of her. But I doubt she'd still get the same pleasure somehow, not from me at least.

She rarely touches me anymore. Even when we do have sex we hardly touch. Our fucking has become a forlorn, perfunctory act, performed on the desolate shores of nostalgia. (If that sounds corny, with imagery borrowed entirely from Hollywood, so be it. How else can I express it?)

Most likely Julia will soon return to the kitchen. I decide to load the dishwasher and tidy up the benches, despite our standoff.

I don one of Julia's aprons, struggle into rubber gloves and begin to fill the sink, squirting in far too much detergent, as if I'm putting out a spot fire. Soon I'm up to my elbows in foam, noisily washing pots and pans.

My intention is twofold: first, a petty recrimination to make her feel guilty for her impatience with me, which seemed out of all proportion for a morning exchange over breakfast, and secondly to be consistent with my attitude towards birthdays.

Good, you're finally cleaning up in here, she says, returning.

I grip the edge of the sink, close my eyes, and shake my head. *Since when have I never cleaned up after your friends?* But I've failed to detect her humour. The petulant mood has passed and she's returned to cheer me, to consolidate our fragile camaraderie.

My work colleagues, Frank.

Your community?

Yes, if you want to put it that way.

And herein lies a difference. A journalist—a good journalist, at least—is an observer of the community, a natural outsider, who, to be of service to the community, sacrifices his place within it.

She hugs me and kisses my temple. *Don't be such an old grump.* She pats my bum and moves away to allow me to continue with the chores.

Two words—*old grump*—have a demoralising effect. And the physical contact makes me suspect a pre-emptive guilty conscience. She's finding it difficult to contain her cheerfulness, genuinely trying to avoid offending me. After all there is still some sedimentary affection between us. I have given her no reason to hate me, to discard me completely. *I wish you'd soaked these pots after you used them last night,* I say, scrubbing and grumping.

Oh, come on, Frank, why didn't you? I did the cooking.

Without responding I scrub some more, suspecting I'm the only writer in the world who does the dishes. The thought depresses me.

I'll get out of your way then, she suggests. *Have a good day, mate.*

Mate? Really? What's happened to darling, sweethcart, even sweetie pie?

Before she departs there's a knock at the door. She's quick to call *I'll get it.* Who was she expecting or fearing might show up?

I stop scouring the fry pan and listen to her footsteps go down the passage. Perhaps this is her date—sorry, friend—sorry, colleague—whatever. She removes the security snippet and unlocks the door, which I keep locked even during the day when we're home, a habit I've developed, since, like other journalists, I've garnered a few enemies over the years. But it annoys Julia who feels she's living in a fortress, unnecessarily and undesired, a minor point of periodic contention.

Oh, good morning. Can I help you? Her tone suggests the visitor is a stranger, her question slightly ridiculous, superfluous, since surely a stranger wouldn't knock without a request, although I admit I've asked it often enough myself when someone unknown knocks on the door.

The response comes in a deep timbre that carries unmistakable authority. *Does Frank Munro live here?*

I sense Julia looking back along the passage before answering. *What's the problem, officer?*

I expect to hear of another recent death. But who? I have no close relatives that I'm still talking to. *We've had a complaint.*

A dramatic pause that Julia is most adept at. *Against Frank? There must be some mistake.*

I detect a throaty sound of constrained cynicism. *If he's home, can we have a word with him please?*

Sure, come in.

There are footsteps approaching. I rush to remove my gloves. No time for the apron but relieved I've removed the fez, I see Julia looking at me, eyebrows arched like duelling Sydney Harbour Bridges, quizzical head extended towards me, a hand clasping together the lapels of her dressing gown in a show of modesty, as she steps aside to allow two police officers to enter.

Frank Munro?

I make a gesture intended to convey sincerity and by inference my law-abiding proclivities. *Good morning.* My tone is replete with puzzlement.

The officer removes her hat, as part of police protocol or out of respect for male undertaking domestic duties, I can't tell. The junior officer behind her, a pimply-faced, thin-lipped lad who looks like he should still be at school, doesn't follow her example, probably needy of the authority his cap confers.

Do you know Dr Stanley Herbert-Jones?

My turn to display the Sydney Harbour Bridges, in a moment of reflection. *Our neighbour,* I say with a slight frown. *He lives next door,* I add unnecessarily, slipping out of the apron. My expression changes to concern. *Is he okay?*

The movement of eyebrows is contagious. It's the officer's turn. *He claims you assaulted him this morning.*

My eyebrows. *I beg your pardon? I what?*

I detect a smirk. One eyebrow. And the corners of her mouth turn slightly. A promising sign. *With a garden hose. That is, you turned a hose on him. You doused him. Allegedly.*

I look from the officer to Julia and back, trying for incredulity. *Why on earth would I do that?*

The officer smiles, having heard these lines performed by countless amateurs before. *Perhaps you can tell me.*

I pause, frowning, thinking. *Officer, I don't know if I should be saying this, but the doctor had to retire last year.* I give Julia an extended look, as if seeking her approval to continue with the sensitive information I'm about to divulge, although she can't possibly know what I might say. *His practice, you know, had been going downhill for some time due to—how can I put this delicately?—a deterioration in his mental faculties, bad diagnoses, even unprofessional behaviour with female clients, et cetera. He's also facing several negligence lawsuits. Look, don't get me wrong he's a lovely man, but—*I leave unsaid my accusation, allowing the police officer to draw her own conclusions.

Curious to see how Julia is coping, not only with the indignity of having the police in her kitchen on my account, but with a husband, expert in the art of obfuscation, commit an informal kind of perjury. I cast a furtive eye in her direction and am grateful she has made an effort to conceal her fury, which I'm able to detect with the benefit of countless hours of enforced experience deciphering her moods.

She gives a little cough. *I can't imagine Frank doing something like that. He goes a bit crazy with the hose sometimes. We have a big garden. Did you notice? Of course you would've, you're police officers. Trained to be observant,* she adds unnecessarily. *Maybe he sprayed the poor doctor by accident. The old fellow's often prowling along our fence line. Frank might've slipped. He's not the steadiest bloke on his feet these days, on account of his weight problem. As you can see, his health's not the best.*

I gape at her in wonder as she comes to my defence, when my arrest and incarceration would best suit her immediate plans. It's such an ingenious response. She points out my weight problem when I'm least able to protest. Defence and attack in the one bundle. And it's not just me in her sights. More than once the doctor has made lewd suggestions to her across the adjoining fence. *He's an old perv,* she's told me. *But he's clever about it. Never says anything direct but I know what he wants.* Which, of course, is one of a myriad reasons I was careless with the hose.

The junior officer coughs, a technique for entering the conversation. *Why water the garden when it rained heavily last night?* As soon as he speaks he shuffles self-consciously, wondering if he's spoken out of turn.

Not heavily enough for our thirsty plants, constable, I say, too quickly. *The subsoil is bone dry.*

The senior officer raises one eyebrow at her colleague and signals their departure with a nod. *Perhaps a bit more care with the hose and an apology wouldn't go astray,* she says as they head for the front door.

Of course, officer.

Not to that old bugger, Julia mutters after they are out of earshot.

I sense an allegiance and realise it has always been there, for many years at least, activating like an old treaty whenever one of us is under siege. It was negotiated in a different era and it's not unconditional but occasionally I get to see its benefits.

Julia pauses as she passes the kitchen door on her way somewhere deeper into the house. *You should have known the silly old prick would cause trouble,* she chastises and is gone, depriving me of the opportunity to defend myself, which would have been difficult, requiring a convoluted answer that may have drawn on her own unpleasant experiences with the neighbour, who frankly has always found some way to annoy us.

I didn't know wetting someone was a crime? I shout as I slip back into the apron and gloves and return to the sink. *And I'm no more overweight than you!*

The dish water is lukewarm thanks to the annoying inquisition. I remove the plug and while the sink is draining I stare vacantly through the kitchen window. There is a path between our house and the side fence and something similar beyond it. What I see angers me.

Lately, anger is an emotion that bubbles up for no apparent reason, although here the reason is obvious. I detect two white caps above the palings and realise the officers have gone to report back to the doctor.

I open the window furtively to eavesdrop. The senior officer, her voice with its unmistakeable no-nonsense sonority, tells the doctor his complaint is going nowhere. *Unless you have evidence of intent, it's your word against his, I'm afraid.*

I can't see the doctor, except perhaps some gossamer hair that wafts in exasperation above the fence line. *My word must be worth something in a court of law, I'm a doctor.*

That's not how the justice system works in this country, Doctor.

Well, it damn-well should.

If you have any more trouble, don't hesitate to contact us.

The gossamer hair rises again. *What's the bloody point?*

My anger vanishes like water spilt onto our parched garden. I punch the air and commence a little jig. In a more robust mood, I refill the sink, finish the greasy pots and pans, turn on the dishwasher, wipe down the benches, collect up the condiments and the dinner mats from the dining room table and put them in the appropriate storage space. Finally, I collect the empty wine bottles and take them outside through our side door, onto the narrow path. I drop them into the recycle bin from a height. They clatter. Is that a curse I hear emanating from the bowels of our neighbour's abode?

Inside again, I inspect my work, to ensure it measures up to Julia's exacting standards. A few specks of masticated food mark the dining-room table, the remnants of Professor George Somebody's intellectual flourishes, which I remove with a disposable cloth.

I slip off the gloves, hang up the apron and head for the bathroom, feeling light-headed because something has finally happened in my favour.

My levity lasts until I stand before the mirror, which is lit too luridly, highlighting my blepharitis. I look ghoulish. I suspect it has clairvoyant attributes, projecting an image from a decade into the future. My first senile wart, a grey protrusion, located where the Devil has one of his horns, appears to be growing. I half expect another to pop up on the other side of my forehead any time soon for balance. There are other flatter blemishes on my pate, three sun spots, two blood spots on the temples, spider veins on the cheeks, due to an excessive consumption of red wine according to Julia, some eczema on the throat and a cluster of blackheads on the side of the nostrils, which I'm certain weren't there yesterday.

I run the hot water to dampen a flannel and lean towards the mirror for a closer inspection. Definitely blackheads despite my regular ablutions. After applying the steaming flannel to open the pores, I squeeze them out, which leaves the skin red and angry. Now there are little holes instead of blackheads which I hope will close in the next minute or two, but I know will never close entirely and will be vulnerable to further deposits of grime.

My skin is no longer as elastic as it used to be. Not exactly leathery, not papery, not mummified yet, it retains some suppleness, which allows me room for hope that my youth has not entirely deserted me. Sometimes when I look in mirrors I'm shocked by what I see. It makes me think that mirrors are no longer manufactured to the standards they used to be. The same applies to the modern camera, digital photography, which flattens out my features and makes me appear ancient. Where is that agreeable fellow I see in the photos of yesteryear? That's what my mind settles upon when I'm not in front of a mirror. Surely I can't have become this ugly. But ugliness is what I see.

Do others see it? Surely it's the mirror, the camera. It dismays me because I'm cynical enough to believe our initial judgment of others is based almost entirely on appearance. We might modify our opinions as we get to know them, but find it difficult to abandon the initial appraisal, no matter how inappropriate it is.

Take my dead friend, Charlie, who had a tumour under one cheek, which made his face look lopsided. It was hardly noticeable while he wore his glasses, but if he took them off or when he was weary after hours of reading, where the left jowl seemed to sag as well, with his thick glasses slipping awkwardly down his nose, the lopsidedness was stark, and together with his myopia, led me to think of him as lopsided in many respects, including his thinking.

I remember our first serious discussion was about the Cuban Revolution at a dinner party that Julia had arranged, shortly after she had met him at a public campaign rally. I don't recall how the topic arose, except that Cuba was a country he had recently visited in support of its revolution, which he considered an ongoing affair more than thirty years after the overthrow of the tyrant Batista. Having been an international journalist, I listened with interest. He was talking at length and in great detail on its history, until he mentioned the execution of *counter-revolutionaries,* on the orders of the legendary guerrilla leader whose image was on the T-shirt that Charlie had just gifted me, at which point I interrupted and suggested that such unnecessary brutality was unworthy of the socialist ideal. *A certain amount of repression was necessary to ensure the revolution triumphed,* he responded, to which I declared, *The rot sets in early.* Given that Cuba continued to jail political opponents and others it didn't like, I felt vindicated in my judgment of Charlie, lopsided in looks, lopsided in thought, an attitude I struggled to change as I got to know him better, eventually admitting he was a decent man, despite our differences on the necessity of violence to change the world.

I notice hairs growing from my ears. I pull them out quite regularly with tweezers rather than trimming them with scissors to avoid creating a mass of dark growth, as dense as coastal scrub, a thicket you see in the ears of some men my age. It's pure vanity, of course, to want the hair removed, since it's as natural as shoulder and back hair. But nature is something we've come to disdain. I'm plucking them, enduring the little stabs of pain, when Julia, fully dressed, rushes in.

Sorry, she cries, as she struggles with her dress, hastens out of her underwear and drops onto the toilet. *I couldn't make it back upstairs.*

I suspend the forensic foray into my ears, press both hands onto the vanity basin and lower my head. A stench assails me.

Christ, I mutter.

Must have been the prawns, she gripes.

One side of my mouth rises in a sanctimonious smirk. *I told you last night they were off.*

She emits a piercing squeal, much like the sound she makes, I vaguely remember, in orgasm, but I assume it's not pleasure she's experiencing.

I realised the prawns weren't fresh and refused to eat them. But I noticed the professor wolfing them down. I wonder what shape he's in this morning. I allow my imagination to wander. I imagine him clutching the dunny seat with both hands, lips stretched wide by invisible hooks, evaluating the price one pays for dalliance.

What are you grinning at?

Am I? I glance at her pained expression via the mirror. *I was just thinking how close we've become over the years.*

She unravels a copious amount of toilet paper. Tears it off. *Can you look away?*

My head tilts back and my jaw drops, forming a gaping orifice of faux incredulity. *So there are boundaries.*

It's meant to be facetious but she's indignant. *Of course there bloody well are. You know that. You stopped plucking your bloody ears when I came in, for instance.*

She finishes wiping her bum, stands to pull up her underwear, and flushes. That's when I notice she's wearing scanty red knickers resembling the ones I bought her for a birthday a few years ago, hoping it might revitalise our flagging sex life, the ones she refused to wear and had tossed into a bag of discarded clothes intended for a charity store, accusing me of buying myself a present.

I'm unable to disguise my alarm. *I thought you got rid of those?*

What, these panties? I changed my mind and kept them for a rainy day.

I utter a noise that's meant to signify my indignation but sounds supercilious. *And so it's raining today, is it?*

She frowns, disliking my tone. *I've run out of clean undies is what I mean. I've been too busy this week to do my laundry. I thought now you're not working so much you might help me with that.*

She has a surfeit of everything else in her wardrobe but not underwear, apparently. Only this purpose-specific pair.

I wish you wouldn't make such a mess of the vanity basin. She moans, allowing frustration to creep into her voice, as if she has told me a dozen times before, which she has, unnecessarily, because I always wipe up the shaving slops in my own time. *Oh, Frank, Frank, how often do I have to remind you?*

I'm convinced it's a diversion. It heightens my suspicion. *You know I'm the one who always cleans it up, even on my birthday,* I reply, angling for her conscience.

She moves close to me at the mirror, her dress—a new one by the look of it—re-adjusted, inspecting the lipstick she must have applied elsewhere, puckering her lips, making some modifications with her pinkie.

You're rather tarted up for someone going to help out a uni mate with his thesis, aren't you?

Her pucker freezes for a moment. *Frank, you know I hate that word. Tart. It's so sexist. Anyway, I told you I'm seeing Mum as well but you don't seem to listen to me these days.* She looks away, her eyelids fluttering as if she regrets the sudden shift from accusation to explanation, making her appear guileful.

You deliberately never dress up for your mother. It's always trackie dacks and hoodie, like some western suburbs' bogan. She won't look at me. *Given up on provoking her, have you?* I swish the razor around in the tepid water and tap it crossly against the porcelain basin. With my head bowed I raise an eyebrow to observe her.

We're going out. A minor grimace transforms her expression.

You and your mother or you and this uni student?

Mum of course! She's getting crosser.

Can't tell me where? Both my eyebrows activate now, arching in a world-weary manner.

Why the inquisition? she demands but seeing my righteous expression, my raised eyebrows and pursed lips, decides an explanation is less adversarial. *I don't know yet, it's her choice. Maybe some shopping. Maybe we'll go check out the lingerie at Myers. Stock up a bit. Ha, ha.*

Excellent idea. Then you won't need those others for a rainy day. You can dispense with them.

Over the years I've been so unfair to Mum, it's about time I did some things on her terms. After all, I owe her my whole existence.

Half of it, I correct.

She's close to the mirror, staring at her blemishes and wrinkles, with a ruthless detachment. *It's just a pity you didn't reconcile with your mother before she died. You and I, Frank, have been really selfish over the years, just thinking of ourselves, you with your career, me, well, with my academic studies and my community involvement, taking our parents for granted, hurting them with our indifference, while we muddled along, making the same mistakes they probably made. I'm ready to listen to her more and to do a few things that she'd like to do with her daughter, before it's too late.*

Her tone is sincere and accusatory. Suddenly I feel ashamed. She has reminded me of the passing years, the years together, each year, each day, each hour, each minute nibbling away at our lives together, unnoticed, until the whole caboodle is threatened.

By what? Familiarity? Boredom? Oneness? All white ants!

I'll be staying over tonight.

As she moves away from the mirror I lean towards it to examine the quality of my shaving, which is below par around the jaw where the whiskers are toughest. *Fair enough,*

I say, repressing a desire to continue the interrogation about her attire, which still strikes me as more suitable to a romantic liaison than a family reunion.

Mum'll appreciate the effort I've made. She gives me an affectionate peck on the side of the head and tugs one of my ears. *You've missed a few hairs, by the way. Down inside. You probably can't see them.*

She chuckles as she departs with a flourish of her new dress, displaying no sign of the tension between us. She has a callous sense of humour, which I admire, always have, even when I'm the target. It's a strength, wouldn't you say? If there's adversity on the horizon she marches rather than crawls towards it.

Got a little overnight bag packed, have we? I call. *Don't forget your PJs.*

Won't be needing them. She paused long enough for the implication to mess with my mind. *There'll be a spare nightie, I'm sure.*

Where? My voice is shrill.

At Mum's! God, Frank, where did you think I meant? By the way, what's it like outside? Will I need an umbrella? she calls from afar. *One of our neighbours has been complaining about how wet it's been.*

Despite my dismay, I chuckle. *Just a localised shower* is my rejoinder, although I doubt she's listening.

■

At the sound of the front door closing, I pause a few moments, as silence descends on the house. Then I drop my pants and stare at my old boy in the mirror. He appears slightly larger there than he ever does looking directly down at him, the only time I give the mirror credit, but reflection or otherwise he's always struck me as uninspiring, certainly no match for the tantric dick I saw. But no woman has ever complained. He has never strayed far, not as far as he would have liked, on account of my unwillingness to risk losing Julia, and certainly not as far as some male journalists I know, who claim dozens of *conquests*, as they call them. All things considered, Julia should be grateful for my restraint.

I address my dick. *I believe you, too, are about to be made redundant.*

I take my shaving brush and lather him. I'm not shaving down there. I'm lubricating. The brush tickles a little, a pleasant sensation. I swap it for my hand, squeeze and pull, until my blood responds.

I think of Julia in her new dress. She looked so damn sensual. But not for my benefit. Which doesn't progress my cause. It'll have to be Chloe Dukakis. I close my eyes and allow her to materialise. She steps out of the shadows, beautiful, lascivious, to lean against the vanity basin. Her legs part and I can see the dark mound beneath pink filigree panties. Her fingers pull the material aside.

Good God, already I've convulsed. A bewildering, anticlimactic outcome.

I feel cheated. All mess and no reward. I wanted the build-up, the tremendous pressure, the asphyxiating anticipation of release, where all thought is stifled and the body flows electric. Instead it's already in the basin, the vanity basin, a viscid jet of off-white fluid, the start of life—but not this time.

An empty gesture. *Happy birthday, Frank.*

A sensation like nausea overwhelms me. Recently I read that our secrets define us. I wonder if this defines me. The pejorative term Julia would use is *wanker*. Are all men the same? Do other men my age do this? I admit, I wouldn't have the courage to ask.

I wash the soap from my flushed cheeks and sagging dick, pat them dry with a hand towel, and commence the rest of my ablutions, armpits, corners of the eyes, teeth, trying to forget what I've just done.

There are bags beneath my eyes. My mouth is down-turned; these days its latent state. A tragic-comic look. I try a smile but it appears false. I pull up my pants, tuck myself in, turn off the light and leave the bathroom.

The house is silent. It loses something of its character when Julia is absent. I often turn on the radio to fill the void, not the old fashioned Bakelite contraption I removed from a waste-collection pick-up in the neighbourhood, which Julia soon banished to the tool shed, the only place I can listen to it, but a modern digital receiver incorporated into a sound system she bought at great expense for sonic qualities she insists are required to properly appreciate modern record-ings and do justice to all the hard-working, underpaid, under-valued musicians to whom she listens. It is in the living room near my preferred armchair.

I avoid listening to the news again. Gardening programs, pet advice, medical advice and house-repair tips pervade the AM airways on Saturday mornings. I search for the classical music station on the FM band. Some static, then Mozart. Definitely Mozart. I know that much. Perfect. Maybe one of his piano concertos. I can't tell for sure. There is a faint smell of sandalwood in the air, reminding me of a time when Julia kept sachets of the stuff in the bedroom to enhance our love making. She doesn't do it now but I have no recollection of when she stopped. Mozart. Forget about Julia for a while.

Julia scoffed at me recently for being a hypocrite, which at the time I felt was unjust and spiteful, one of her attempts to undermine our relationship. *Why do you get angry at me when I drive over the speed limit?* she asked.

I had a pat moralising answer. *You're forgetting my near-fatal road accident was due to some fool speeding.*

She allowed me a moment of sanctimonious breathing. *So why were you speeding yesterday when we were going to see my mother?*

I knew she was right but I denied it. She countered with evidence: the exact place my misdemeanour occurred and the speed I was travelling.

Well, if I did, it was unintentional, I said, aggrieved. *Why didn't you warn me? You know I'm dead against it.*

Her chuckle was unsympathetic. *You're lying, Frank. I saw you glancing at the speedometer three times.*

I made some exasperated noises that sounded like I was trying to dislodge a sticky biscuit from my palate. *We were running late to meet your damn mother, that's why.*

Something died between us. *Don't blame her, Frank, that's cowardly. You're the one obsessed with punctuality.*

What are you calling me, a hypocrite? My eyes widened to express my hurt.

She didn't answer directly but presented more evidence. *I know how outraged you get when someone jumps a queue. Yet last time we went to the movies you pushed in to buy tickets, remember?*

I stared at her, incredulous. *Our movie was about to start. I'm sure no one minded. They were most likely buying tickets for one of the other movies that started later than ours.*

I could see my argument hadn't persuaded her.

How do you know that?

I threw up my hands in dismay, mystified by her attack. *Well—well—were they panicking? Were they annoyed?* I stammered.

You deliberately avoided looking at any of them to see how they reacted.

I gestured for a fair hearing. *We were in a hurry! You know I hate missing the start of movies. A few weren't happy about it, I agree.*

How do you know?

They muttered at me.

Her laughter was merciless. *I rest my case.*

I left my armchair and headed for the door, raised my voice. *What, I'm on trial now, am I?*

I caught a glimpse of her nodding.

Mozart. Perfection. Listen to it. Absorb it.

On the side table next to my armchair there is an old framed photo of me, seated on a cane chair with Julia on my lap with an arm around my shoulders. It was taken on the verandah of a farmhouse we rented for a while to see how we liked the country lifestyle. We had no intention of farming, but there were agisted cattle in the surrounding paddocks, which lent our aspirations authenticity. We had been together for a few years and were heading for our thirties. In the photo both of us radiate happiness. But more. We radiate a precocious confidence, as if enlightenment was just over the rise where the cattle went each evening. It must have been taken not long after our arrival because before the year was up we were living back in Melbourne, unable to endure the isolation, missing our friends who had promised to visit but seldom did, pissed off with poor TV reception, unnerved by the night silence, intimidated by a Milky Way free of city glare, a billion stars all with the possibility of life circling around them to remind us of our insignificance.

I stare at the photo. Suddenly I'm crying. I sink into the comfort of my armchair and wail like an abandoned hound. Regret surges through me, deflates me, voids me.

How long it lasts is unimportant. Minutes, maybe hours, pass. It takes me by surprise. I haven't wept so openly in years. Must be feeling fragile from all the dinner-party drinking.

I feel soft afterwards. Cleansed. But of what I cannot say.

I turn off the radio and stay seated, unwilling to move or think, allowing the sensation to wash over me. Mozart is gone. Gradually my breathing steadies. I become aware of another sound. A clock. An heirloom. A grandfather clock in our hall. Inherited from my father when my siblings refused to take it. Its regular tempo projects authority. Each beat a warning, an admonishment, an exhortation, gone as soon as it arrives. I have no way of stopping it, even for a moment.

 I move before it strikes ten.

What shall I do for my birthday? Nothing? It's just another day. Perhaps a movie. It would've been nice if Julia had suggested that. I can't exactly remember the last time we went to the movies together. Maybe after the queue incident.

I feel bloated. It's the pikelets she fed me. And yet, because I skipped my usual breakfast, I have an urge to eat more before I go anywhere. A normal breakfast. Out of habit.

I resist the temptation although the craving doesn't subside.

In the hall the clock chimes. Fuck, half the morning gone. Almost half my birthday. Julia has gone her merry way and I'm left to put out the rubbish from her dinner party, sweep up the food that never made it into mouths. Amazing where it ends up. Back in the dining room, I find some stuck half-way up the wall two metres from the nearest possible source. Another of Professor What's-his-name's intellectual flourishes no doubt, when he used his fork like a conductor's baton.

I should just leave his stain. Frame it, perhaps. Don't want to be accused of philistinism, or worse, barbarism, acting like some academic version of the Taliban. After all, it symbolises the premise on which his entire argument depended.

I need a proper breakfast. My normal breakfast.

I hunch my shoulders and head for the kitchen. No introspection now, just automatically remove an egg and two rashers from the fridge, the frypan from its hook and head for the stove. I glance at the calendar just to confirm I have been right about the date. I take time to admire its photo, a mossy branch from the rainforest of Tasmania, so remote, so pristine, somewhere Julia's been hiking, with a few of her colleagues if I remember correctly. Soon the gas is alight, the fry pan on, the egg and bacon sizzling. I feel virtuous. It's almost half my normal serve. After all, it's not my stomach that needs provender; I've already had pancakes.

In a few moments I'm staring at an empty plate and I'm forced to consider what I'll do next. Get out of the house. Okay, a movie's a good idea, but it's too early. I could go into the city first, buy myself a pair of shoes, which can be a birthday present, since no-one else is buying me one. I've been promising myself new runners for six months. Julia won't begrudge me spending money on runners. She'd encourage it, in fact, knowing what she thinks of my current footwear, which draws a cynical comment every time we step out together.

I like the sound they make, she remarked about a pair with loose soles. *You'll be able to tap dance with them soon. Why don't you get them mended? And a bit of polish wouldn't go astray.*

She thinks people who can afford it but don't spend money on their clothes and appearance are phonies, pretending they belong to the fag-end of the working class or, more pathetically, bohemia. She reckons it's a form of self-loathing.

Like that Bernard fellow you know, she elaborated. *Doesn't wash, wears rags he buys from Savers, never irons anything, the tooth fairy was still around the last time he brushed his teeth, he mistakes combs for relics his wife brings home from her amateur archaeological digs around the city, smokes dope all day and lives off the earnings of half a dozen rental properties he inherited.*

I attempted a half-hearted defence, since she seemed to be implicating me by association. *But he's sincere enough,* I said.

He likes to pretend he's another revolutionary, like poor old Charlie, she continued, flighty with indignation now, *ready to lead his fellow downtrodden against the capitalist oppressors, never thinking he might be one himself. Never gets out of the armchair. Not once have I seen him at a community protest meeting or a public rally.*

I agree with her and am fairly confident he wouldn't be the last to be stood against a wall come the revolution but he's a genial bloke and, although a tad pompous, a reasonable conversationalist. Is there anything wrong with enjoying his company for half an hour if our paths cross?

At least you don't pretend to be a revolutionary, she added, *despite how careless you are with your clothes. That's one thing in your favour.*

I'm a journalist, I said unnecessarily. *I'm above politics. I listen to all sides, all views, and write about what I hear.*

Half her face rose in a cynical grin. *Whatever.*

I'm in no position to shun a person because he's a hypocrite, whereas Julia would keep any communication to formalities and move on, banish him from her community. Like Charlie she's a person of unwavering principle. And then there's the way she dresses when she visits her mother, although apparently, as of today, that's in the past.

What movie should I see? There's bound to be something of interest at the Nova. Its website is but an app away.

I get up to look for my smart phone. I haven't had it long. Such ready access to the internet still impresses me. I'm a late comer to the twenty-first century. Probably the last journalist in the world to get one. Another red mark against my name, professionally. Often I misplace it. I wander the house looking for it, under cushions in the living room, in my study, in the bedroom, in the bathroom, but can't locate it. There is a moment of panic, which settles into a more pervasive anxiety.

Of late I'm conscious of mislaying things. Keys, books, my favourite pen, etcetera. Why am I so distracted these days? What's happening to my mind? I feel like I'm losing control of it, losing my will. But who knows? Maybe control was always an illusion, another of Sartre's misleading assertions.

I decide to phone Julia and ask her if she's seen the phone.

I ring from the landline in the hallway, opposite the grandfather clock, which is ticking away my life indifferently. Julia sounds annoyed that I have bothered her. There's a lot of background noise and a male voice that could be addressing her. Perhaps she's on public transport. Or a noisy café. I doubt it's a party. Not mid-morning surely. Maybe she's yelling because of the background noise rather than being angry with me.

She suggests I do the obvious: ring my own phone and listen.

Sheepishly, I thank her. I take her advice and am surprised to hear its ring tone close by, a track that Apple offer from their standard selection. On the coat rack near the front door my corduroy jacket is playing the blues.

In the side pocket with used tissues and some coins I find it and text Julia with a weak joke. *If you get this message I'm NOT dead,* an ironic allusion to the declaration of a politician Julia loathed and about whom I wrote satirical articles, which I hope she'll appreciate and think of me fondly. The message flies off in a speech bubble and lodges on my screen.

I stare at the phone, envying it. I have no idea what half its apps are for. What is *Safari*? What is *Face Time*? It's smarter than me. I admit it. I feel deflated. Belittled by my phone. The time will come when a machine like this will be able to think, will be conscious, will be able to reproduce itself. It won't need us. Machines, not humans, will conquer the universe. Time will be no obstacle because the machine is lifeless. What's a million light years to a well-oiled machine? It would just need plenty of gigabytes to store all the photos it would snap along the way.

No doubt there's books written about this stuff already, sci-fi, a genre I last had an interest in when I was a teenager and the plots were about travel between planets. Nothing too sophisticated. Boys' Own stuff. Simple excitement. Goodies and Baddies. The humans (white ones) were the goodies of course. The aliens (various colours, but never white) the baddies.

I don't need to be told that these days plots are more convoluted, that allegory plays a big role in the genre. A plot set in a different time, a different galaxy, a different dimension can really be a clever way of commenting on contemporary earthly woes. But what's the point? Obfuscation? To allow the reader who gets it to feel good about themselves for being clever? I suppose it's a form of gratification and God knows we hanker for that these days.

My phone makes a muted noise like someone trying to suppress an untimely fart. A message from Julia has arrived. No repartee, which would have been reassuring. *Don't forget to empty the kitchen tidy.* No *xo.* Not even a ☺ or a :).

Why hadn't she emptied it before she left? Why was she in such a hurry?

I decide to leave it, throw on my jacket, slip the phone in with the used tissues and coins, and head for the door, disregarding the kitchen tidy. But I detour to check I've turned off the gas, locked the back door and shut the open windows. I return to the bathroom to check my appearance and tighten the taps. The shower is dripping. I exhale slowly. This vindicates my diligence. I screw the tap to a point I know I'll have trouble undoing it. Run my hand under the rose a few times to ensure the dripping has stopped, unwilling to trust my eyes. I must buy some replacement washers next time I'm near a hardware store. Back to the kitchen to check the taps there, run my hand underneath a few times, no leaks, look at the gas again, notice I've left my plate on the table and slip it into the dishwasher, look at the tidy and mutter *fuck you.*

◼

The front entrance has three locks. An orthodox front door lock, a deadlock, a security door. My keys are on a small chain attached to a leather pouch, in which I keep my small change, although there's always a few stray coins in the pockets of trousers and jackets. There's also a spare set of keys outside in a sealed tin under a statuette of Buddha that Julia is fond of, in case I lose mine.

I set the burglar alarm, step out and lock up, mildly confident that I'm leaving the house in good order. Except for the kitchen tidy. A chill wind has blown in from the bay. I button up my jacket and wish that I'd worn a hat. I only remember now, with the punitive air upon my pate, that I once wore beanies on days like this. These days, however, I wear hats with a bit more style. A fez around the house. Down the street the karakul hat I picked on assignment in Kabul years ago.

Indecision transfixes me. Do I unlock everything to get it or do I suffer a cold head for the rest of the day, which will affect my thinking, my mood? And now that I'm thinking about the cold I decide I also need a scarf.

Hearing the doctor shuffling along his path, I stay out of sight on the porch. He's in a quilted parka, the type you might wear in Scandinavia, and has a fur hat that gives him the air of a Russian aristocrat, like he's just stepped out of a Dostoevsky novel, *The Idiot*, perhaps, or *The Possessed*. He's on the way out and I don't want to seem to be following him down the street. So the decision about the hat and scarf is made easy.

I unlock everything, hasten to the alarm to exploit that ten seconds of grace before I disturb the entire neighbourhood, including the doctor, who is the last person I want to irritate, lest he use the occasion to lure the police back to my doorstep. *Crime and Punishment.*

The search begins. The karakul is on our hat stand in the hall but I have trouble locating my favourite scarf. I last wore it a few days ago, and I can't recall where I put it. I have three others: a multi-coloured striped one my mother knitted with acrylic wool before she died, which I refuse to wear and should just give to a charity store but guilt and superstition—yes, I confess, superstition—prevent me; there's a black silk scarf, which I keep for formal occasions when I don a suit; and there's my red and blue Demons footy scarf, which I haven't worn since the club's thirty goal loss to Geelong several years ago. But the one I'm looking for is the long, ribbed, beige, woollen scarf that Julia bought me for one of our anniversaries, although I've forgotten which one, a long time ago—must have been the seventh wedding—no, no, no, we're not married.

Just last year she wrapped it around my neck, in a noose-like fashion, and told me I looked handsome *in a rough, manly kind of way.* I tried to show my appreciation with a rough, manly kiss, but she turned her face deftly, permitting only a peck on the cheek.

I see meaning in many things, particularly the slightest of gestures. I don't mind affection but I grieve the loss of passion.

I wore our little symbol during a recent cold spell, so I look in places where I might have left it inadvertently, in all my drawers and cupboards, on the bench by the back door, in the bedroom, where on cold nights I am sometimes known to wrap it around my head. In frustration I rifle through the bedroom drawers, her drawers. It's not there, of course, but I find several pairs of her panties! Weren't they supposed to be in the wash?

I'm shaken by the deceit. It's so out of character for her to lie to me. I take a pair and slump onto the edge of the bed and hold them to my face. They smell of fabric softener. I wonder what the red ones smell of. *Julia*, I moan, *what's become of us?* It takes five minutes to convince myself it was just an oversight rather than something duplicitous.

The last place I look for the scarf is in my dirty-clothes basket.

And there it is.

I recall her complaints about its odour last time I wore it. I sniff it now and have to admit it is slightly rancid, which doesn't bother me but I'm prepared to concede it might bother others, especially Julia who has a highly refined sense of smell, an unfortunate talent with which to be overendowed although useful at certain cheap restaurants.

Yet she failed to pick up on the prawns last night. Something must have been distracting her.

As I tie the scarf around my neck in an unfashionable knot, I feel slightly defiant but also bordering on the puerile, given Julia's unilateral decision to toss it in the wash bears all the hallmarks of sound judgment, which I should respect. But what she doesn't know won't hurt her.

I head for the front door, picking up my laptop bag in case I feel like working while I'm out. At the door, I detour back via the kitchen to collect the plastic bag from the tidy, so nothing is left for her to complain about. The cantankerous doctor has had plenty of time to go wherever he's going. I pull on the karakul, adjust its angle in the hall mirror until I appear like a slightly chubby version of the Afghan president, or is that ex-president now?—whose name at the moment escapes me—reset the alarm, lock the doors and step out, glad to be alone, relieved to be embarking on a day where I am in control, without a rigid plan, with only a few competing ideas about my destiny. Nothing too taxing.

Despite the sense of betrayal, there's an ambivalent flush of gratitude for Julia's absence. Where should I head first? Well, there's really only one way for the moment, down our dead-end street (which Julia prefers to call a cul-de-sac) towards the shops on the corner where I can buy a newspaper to read (yes, the one I used to work for, and I almost hear the braying, *masochist* and not the praise, *magnanimous*) while I drink a long black, al fresco, at one of the cafés that have appeared in our neighbourhood in recent years.

The newsagent, an Indian immigrant, is too busy selling tickets in a $20 million dollar draw to greet me. I drop the correct change onto the counter and shuffle out past the queue, where a few of the faces are familiar and one says, *You've got to be in it to win it.* I raise my eyebrows neutrally, pretending to be above such folly, having bought my weekly ticket two days earlier. I turn my attention to the headlines.

Nothing about the massacre in Paris. It's a long time since the news has reached us first in print. I flick through the pages but don't find the article I submitted on the hypocrisy of the government's immigration policy. I consider myself an expert on hypocrisy but the editor (yes, Dukakis!) has opted for commentary by a leading expert on immigration.

I head along the street to the Lounge Lizard.

The precinct has no trees. It is a busy thoroughfare. A gloomy atmosphere prevails. Still, I sit outside and read while I wait for a waitress to come and take my order. I read from the sports pages. The cricket news. The football season is well and truly over, which is a good thing since I no longer follow the game, unimpressed with the way it's played these days and sick of reading about the continual humiliations of my former team.

There's an alarming noise. A motorbike has shot from the curb into the traffic, causing a car to brake violently. *Fuck!* I shout. The agitation that seizes me seems out of all proportion to the incident. Rising from my chair and after thoughtful reflection, I scream *Dickheads!* towards the bike, whose pillion passenger gives me the bird.

Doesn't she have beautiful hair! declares the waitress who approaches from behind, surprising me.

I twist my neck to look at her. *Who?*

The woman on the back of that bike.

How could you tell? She's in a bloody helmet.

She was in here just now. Lovely red hair. Not sure it's natural but. She comes in here now and then. I thought you knew her, actually. I'm sure I've seen her with you once or twice.

I doubt it. Behaving like an idiot. Didn't you see her give me the bird?

She shrugs. *Maybe you've done something to upset her.*

I don't even know her! I notice my voice sounds hysterical. I flop back onto the chair and look anywhere but at the waitress.

What would you like? Her tone is low and contemptuous. It's sisterhood she's now experiencing.

When I turn towards the waitress I grunt. *A bit of peace and quiet would be a good start.* I'm stiff in the neck. Chronically so. A physio has told me it'll take more than a year to correct itself, even if I follow the exercises he prescribes. The face of the waitress is inanimate. No sign of sympathy whatsoever. *A long black, thanks, love, no sugar.*

Her eyes harden at the affectionate title but she refrains from a retort. Bad for business. And her job is insecure. Her job is casual, like most young people. Gone are the days of a job for life. Ha, ha, we must have been living in Cloud Cuckoo Land when we thought that was the natural order. I watch her go, specifically her shapely legs, at the same time wondering why she thought I would know any bikies or bikie molls (as female pillions have been labelled) for that matter.

I spread the newspaper across the table ready to read.

Frank, how are you, man?

Looking up, annoyed at the interruption, I see a familiar face, grey skinned, eyes and nose ravaged—my guess by a chronic penchant for brandy—stained teeth, billygoat jaw. Jack (aka Jacques) Martin. Still smoking Gauloises and wearing a beret. Went to France twenty-five years ago and returned a few years later as a Chef de Cuisine. Ran a successful restaurant, catering for the business community, until an eminent politician choked to death on a bone from his famous Bordeaux fish fillet dish. I remember writing an article about how the restaurant tried to keep it hush-hush, which is how I discovered he wasn't really French. He could have worked again, in a reduced capacity, perhaps an *escuelerie*, but he lost his nerve.

He still speaks with a faux European accent and uses a curious mixture of foreign and local jargon. *I hate to put the bite on you, mate, but would you mind shouting me a coffee? Je n'ai pas d'argent. Not a brass razoo, mon ami. I'm currently in negotiation with the government.*

I smile urbanely. *Centrelink?*

He nods. *You understand we're at a delicate stage. They claim I never meet my obligations. Twenty job applications a week is cruel and unnecessary punishment, you'd agree, I'm sure, Monsieur Frank, a smart journalist like you.*

Unusual punishment, I correct the legal expression to prove his final point, but he thinks I'm amplifying his complaint.

Absolutely. As soon as—

I gesture towards the seat opposite mine and offer to buy him some toast as well.

He grimaces. *Mate, mate, I would prefer a croissant.*

We've had this conversation before. So have other regulars at the Lounge Lizard and other cafés along this strip. It is how

I know him. He is careful not to overplay the begging with any one customer. He spreads himself around.

The coffee here's good, non? he says, dropping casually onto the seat and signalling to the waitress, who attends and takes his order.

On my bill, I tell her.

He regards me sincerely, nodding appreciation. *You look a little, how can I say this, down in the mouth, Monsieur.* He points to the paper, now folded on one side of the table. *All bad news, is it? This is the reason I never read. Why make my life more miserable than it is already? Life's too short.* He sighs while he caresses his goatee.

I raise an eyebrow, sit back and study him. His composure annoys me. *Haven't you heard what happened in Paris?*

His bloodshot eyes stare back at me, curious. *Quelle?* he says, almost flippantly.

I look away, searching for the waitress, someone positive to view. *There's been a massacre.*

He gapes. *Non? Quand?*

I tell him what I'd heard on the radio.

He reaches for the paper, flicks through the pages. Nothing. He looks confused.

It's only just happened, I explain and feed him some more details.

He tosses the paper aside. *Mon Dieu!* His hands are in the air gesticulating. An iPhone appears in his possession and he's tapping its screen frantically. *Non, non, non! Mon Dieu! Mon Dieu!* He starts to rise and then drops back into his seat, looking around, perhaps for something reassuring, something French.

Fortunately the waitress arrives with the croissant.

Ces fous hommes, ces hommes qui font une moquerie de l'islam, l'amour de la mort, he mutters after tearing a piece of the roll, placing it in his mouth and chewing despairingly.

I have to admit, for someone who only spent a few years in France decades ago, his French is remarkably well-preserved.

They don't respect this beautiful life. He spreads his arms, waving the croissant. *How many were killed, did you say?* He's at his phone again. *More than a hundred! Oh, mon Dieu!* His eyes are moist with emotion. He's flicking through what he can find about the massacre on Facebook. *I don't want to think about this anymore. Tell me something, cheerful.*

I've got to go, Jacques. Sorry to be harbinger of bad news. Seems to be my lot.

As I skulk away there's a chill in the air. I look up and see the sweeps of grey across the firmament. Except for a few invasive Indian Mynahs, as notorious to the avian world as jihadists to ours, there's not another bird in sight.

I adjust my karakul and amble along an unremarkable street to the railway station, an old brick building with timber cornices, a decorative cross, worn stone steps for the sound of body and a bitumen ramp for the rest of us, which makes it a little further to reach the platform, but gentler on the knees. I use its handrail to steady my balance, aware that the slight elevation has my heart working overtime.

The building once housed railway staff who sold tickets and dispensed travel and timetable advice but they are gone, replaced by machines which do their job at substantially lower costs according to the doyens of transport infrastructure, providing the damage done by vandals and thieves and the loss of revenue from fare evaders is ignored.

There are people waiting for the next train, all involved with smart phones, none seated on the platform's metal benches, which are still wet from overnight rain.

The travellers are ignoring me. We are strangers, but their indifference, which seems intentional, leaves me feeling slightly uncomfortable. No acknowledgement of my existence here. Ridiculous to expect it, I know. Nevertheless, uncomfortable is how I remain until I remind myself not everybody is going to be friendly to people they don't know. And why should they know me, even if they've heard of me or read my articles. The tiny photo that sometimes appeared next to what I wrote, taken some ten or fifteen years ago, could hardly identify me. Besides I would also view that sort of friendliness with suspicion, even uneasiness, or alarm in some instances.

Once I witnessed a toothless woman with stains on her dress pass along a platform greeting each person with a salute and the declaration *Nice day!* then offering to shake hands, harmless behaviour by any measure but a flagrant disregard of modern urban sensibilities. I was on the opposite platform so her behaviour didn't threaten me directly, but perhaps it would have if I'd been next in line, for the salutation was a clever trap. There was no escape. Some ignored the greeting and stood stony-faced, staring up the tracks pretending to be looking for the next train, like cold-hearted bastards who cared little for the misfortunes of others, unwilling even to acknowledge her existence but enduring guilt for a few minutes at least. Others reciprocated politely before returning their gaze to the tracks, which was an opening for the derelict to interact. This prospect caused anxiety. What did she want? Not just small talk, surely? Money. It had to be. And what did she want money for? Not food. Not clothes. Not medical or hygiene products. Alcohol? Drugs? Should they have worried about what she wanted it for? Or should they have just handed over the money and dignified her with the freedom to spend it on whatever she liked? But maybe it was not money after all. Maybe it was just the modest affirmation.

The next train is due. Most heads, including mine, are looking along the track. The train approaches the platform on rails that appear buckled. It lurches but doesn't derail and rocks to a halt at the platform.

We travellers move in unison towards the doors, clasping our smartphones, listening to other worlds through earplugs or headphones. The doors slide open at the touch of a button. Inside are more listless travellers with smartphones. Few look at us as we enter. I hasten to a vacant seat by a window before someone else can claim it although peak hour has passed and there's enough seats for everyone. Some try to push past me, but that's not easy these days. Ten seconds transpire. I subside, a bit like a seal on a rock shelf, I admit, attempting to catch my breath. As the new passengers settle the doors shut and the train groans forward. It's never a smooth departure. There's always a little jolt to let you know insufficient funds are allocated to the public transport system, which is neglected in this city of cars (See my article, The Age, June 27, 2008, Walkley Award nomination).

I watch as a tardy traveller dashes onto the platform and waves frantically towards the driver's cabin in a futile, almost comical bid to request the train wait. Her shoulders slump when she realises her exhortation failed.

I watch her as I pass. Our eyes meet momentarily and although I'm sure my facial expression is neutral she pulls an angry face at me as if in response to my amusement. I shake my head, trying to convey that she's mistaken. But she has turned away towards a machine that will announce time-table information when she presses its green button.

A sense of misjudgement prevails. Now a total stranger thinks I'm callous. And I'm powerless to change her opinion. Does it matter? Probably not but I can't overcome the emotional rawness I feel when someone unfairly thinks badly of me. Even after decades in the media I can't get over why anyone would want to think badly of me, although those who know me would be surprised to hear it, seeing me as a thick-skinned, crusty, phlegmatic, old pressman whose girth has increased as a kind of fortification against the slings and arrows.

The question lingers until we reach the next station. I avoid looking at the platform lest another misunderstanding arise. I've forgotten to bring a book to read on the train. So I resort to my smart phone, check my emails, nothing, check Facebook.

Friends have updated their status, invited me to like quaint and amusing YouTube videos, added photos, invited me to events—the usual. I have nothing to add. No-one has wished me happy birthday. Nobody who knows has mentioned it to let others know. Perhaps I should have left that reminder. See how many Facebook friends care.

I'm still browsing when someone drops onto the seat next to me emphatically, unlike any stranger would, except someone with a mental disorder. The grinning face is familiar with its insipid eyes, bulging cheeks and unruly dyed blond hair, but the name that should accompany the face eludes me. I'm transfixed in a moment of panic until it eases and plateaus around embarrassment. Names are one of my weaknesses.

Frank, dear boy, fancy running into you like this! I was just talking to Julia the other day.

That should have been a clue, a prompt.

Yes, now I remember, she's a social worker, or counsellor, or something, an old friend of Julia's with whom she'd reconnected at a Pilates classes. We've encountered her at pubs in our suburb, where we've gone to listen to local musicians, live and free, and I've relied on Julia to remember her name.

She isn't the only one whose name I have trouble remembering. It happens to me all the time, even with people I know well, a great disadvantage for a journalist where greeting by name is almost a tool of the trade, potentially disarming reluctant contacts. It is the one chink in my professional armour.

I have to go through a routine, silently reciting the alphabet while we engage in small talk—*How's the weather? What are you up to? How's work?* (although this last question I use with care)—until a letter prompts the person's name, which I belatedly insert into the conversation to show I haven't forgotten who they are.

I'm implementing this strategy when she says, *You don't remember my name, do you?* She gives me time to prove her wrong but not enough time to complete the alphabet. *It's Susanna*, she says. *Susanna Robinson.* Enjoying my embarrassment, she cackles like an old steam-driven pump starting up.

No, no, I lie. *I do remember, Susanna. It's just that you startled me, dropping onto the seat like that.*

Her body language is telling me it doesn't matter. *It's a malaise, Frank. Researchers are calling it Busy Lifestyle Syndrome. Too much information. Google. Facebook. Smartphones. Not enough time to absorb what we learn. Hence the forgetfulness.* She points at my smartphone to corroborate her assertion.

I'm happy for her to give me an excuse but it's hardly deserving. Busy Lifestyle Syndrome? BLS. Julia obviously hasn't yet told her about my retrenchment.

Unless of course it's more serious, anomic aphasia, for example, which might signal you've got some form of dementia. It'd be a tragedy for someone your age to develop Alzheimer's. Poor Julia!

Indeed. What about poor me? But Susanna is an optimist. Again it's her body language speaking louder than words. She's bouncing around in her seat, turning towards me until her knees are digging into my thigh and her hands are comforting my shoulder and knee. *Of course it might just be absentmindedness, Frank. Or indifference.* And there is a deep guttural admonitory tone to her utterance followed by a guffaw and tight squeeze that almost unnerves me. *Psychopaths generally are bad with names too, unless, of course, the person serves their agenda. Nice exotic hat you're wearing, by the way.*

Her phone rings, a dial tone that shrieks *Pick up, granny, pick up!* I don't know what to make of that. Nor do other passengers who've heard the desperate cry. *Are you a granny?* I ask.

Yeah, no, nearly. It's hilarious, don't you think?

You, a granny, or the ring tone?

She abandons my knee and shoulder and turns back into her seat to fossick in a cavernous leather bag until she fetches the beseeching phone. *Hi, honey, what's up?* Her voice has an insouciant lilt.

A hiatus ensues with only a garbled sound reaching me. As she listens her expression fluctuates. A frown is followed by raised eyebrows followed by another frown followed by rolling eyes followed by histrionic gritted teeth and histrionic sigh.

Oh, for God's sake, Donna – she mouths *my daughter* to me – *it's just a heightened terror alert, not a specific threat about the 10.57 Upfield to Flinders Street! And no,* she makes a show of looking around, craning her neck, *I cannot see a bearded Arab in a suicide vest, although I haven't been paying that much attention. Perhaps he's in the next carriage, so I should be all right.*

She hits the red phone button and ends the call. *Honestly, my daughter! She's totally stressed by this terrorist stuff.*

She rolls her eyes but her face is flushed, realising her phone call had gone viral at least in a localised sense, since many of the passengers in our carriage are watching her. *Sorry, sorry. Hey, none of you are wearing suicide vests, are you? No? Thank God for that. Or is it Allah we should thank?* She is kneeling on her seat now, fingers gripping the headrest instead of my knee, looking around the carriage for mirthful responses.

She drops back onto the seat and groans, gripping my leg again. *O-oh, there's a few Muslims back there, a couple of women in hijabs next to a stern looking bloke. Perhaps I shouldn't have said that. They probably found it offensive.* She twists her head, again calls, *Sorry! Sorry!* and then turns back to me. *Where's everyone's sense of humour gone? You know what I hate most about this terrorist stuff? It's totally out of proportion.*

I have to admit, although not to her, I become uneasy when a young bearded Muslim carrying a backpack sits near me on the train. I don't shift, out of cultural sensitivity, but I'm relieved when he or I step out of the carriage in one piece.

You know how many people are killed on the roads each year in this country? she continues. *Yeah, literally hundreds. And how many are killed by terrorists? Any? Okay, just one or two. But why isn't there a state of emergency called for the carnage on our roads? Why aren't people freaking out over that? Why are people still going anywhere near a road?*

I try to avoid roads as much as possible, but I keep my own counsel.

Every year there's more people killed by trains than terrorists.

Suddenly I become unnecessarily conscious of the train I'm on. It rolls and groans along poorly maintained tracks.

What about youth suicide numbers? Why isn't there a state of emergency for our youth? Not that what's happened in France isn't shocking. It is. What's your opinion, Frank?

I'm taken off guard. I didn't expect her to end in anything but a rhetorical flourish. Yet here she is, asking my opinion, sounding me out, as if she were open to contradiction or at least revision. I find this refreshing but also a little unnerving, for what I say might commence a whole new tirade of possible ways to die.

We are approaching another station and that seems to subdue her. *Frank, what's your opinion?* she repeats, although she's more interested in people on the platform.

Well–I begin, but she waves my answer off.

It doesn't matter. She is staring at a group as the train rolls past and comes to a stop. *I love the way those youngsters are dressed. Look at those colours! Look, one of them's got a cap like yours. Cute!*

I peer through the train window whose transparency is impaired by dust and grime and a delinquent's tag and see a group of self-conscious teenagers dressed like medieval jesters. Self-conscious because they are over-acting, gesticulating flamboyantly, pulling grotesque faces, one is even doing backflips. But they aren't completely comfortable with their behaviour. There's sly glances around to see how others are reacting, and they are pleased to see most are enjoying the spectacle.

Are suicide bombers included in our suicide statistics? I say.

Susanna turns away from the window and looks at me sharply. *Oh, very droll, Frank. There's no suicide bombers in Australia. And you know why? There's too much to live for here. Everyone knows they're on a good wicket compared to those other wretched countries.*

Life is short enough without killing yourself, she adds. *Look at them.* She turns her attention again to the colourful youngsters. *'Joie de vivre, Frank, that's joie de vivre. We should all still be feeling that.*

I'm wondering if all the French I'm hearing this morning has something to do with the Paris atrocities, issuing from the collective unconsciousness to which Julia sometimes refers.

At the last moment the merry pranksters rush onto the train, into our carriage. They dance and sing along the aisle. Susanna cheers and high-fives a few as they pass. One reaches over to high-five me but changes his mind when he realises I have no intention of reciprocating, despite both of us wearing karakuls.

Oh, you're such an old fuddy-duddy, Susanna chides. *Do you get enjoyment out of anything?*

Fuddy-duddy? Julia called me that just this morning! Cautiously, I shrug.

I thought not. Poor Julia.

I'm starting to get annoyed by her presumptuousness. She hardly knows Julia, much less me. Her phone beeps, a text, and she settles into her seat to respond.

Mercifully we pass through two stations without another word. Her phone takes precedence. Alongside the railway I observe the zoo, one of our better prisons, but still depressing. I once saw a spider monkey that must have escaped from here run across six lanes of traffic into the garden of a Victorian tenement on Flemington Road. I wrote a short quirky piece about it that made the front page: *Cheeky escapee makes monkey of authorities.* That grabbed the readers' attention.

The next station, Flemington Bridge, is above the entrance to the Tullamarine Freeway, which has no right to the title since it became a tollway decades ago. All the state owned enterprises that used to operate when I was a kid—banks, gas and electricity utilities, public transport, telecommunications—have all been sold off like the Freeway, much to the dismay of people like my dead friend, Charlie, who thought the State was the proper provider of essential services. Now and then he urged me to write articles about their decline under private enterprise and the way promised price reductions never eventuated, how every year prices were hiked above the inflation rate, increasing company margins, which I did write about once or twice with genuine feeling since my bills were crippling me, although I knew it to be a lost cause. You might as well build sand castles to restrain a tsunami. Every time I scrutinised the fine print and saw the cost per kilowatt-hour had soared I was in accord with Charlie on the need for revolution.

I know these thoughts have come into my head because we are approaching Macaulay Station, which lies beneath another tollway, Citylink, an elongated arc that eventually spans the Yarra and curls down under the river and into the south-eastern suburbs. At Macaulay it forms a great concrete ceiling over the platforms.

Whenever I pass through the station I think of my friend, Charlie, who lived nearby and often caught the train. Despite my secular proclivities I feel his presence each time and imagine him standing in his moth-eaten greatcoat, his dirty runners letting the wind chill his toes where synthetic soles and leather uppers have parted company, his lopsided face, his glasses smeared with fingerprints.

The sensation prompts me to look along the platform although I don't really expect to see him. Even as a child I've never believed in ghosts, notwithstanding occasional bouts of superstition. But today the sensation is more poignant. Last night's sentimentality hasn't left me completely. One year on. Charlie is one year into eternity, whatever that might mean.

Shadows fall over us as the train moves under the tollway and rolls towards Macaulay Station. The adjacent bike track and concreted Moonee Valley Creek are in need of maintenance and tidying up. Rubbish lies everywhere. Susanna slips her phone out of sight and recommences her conversation. *Sorry about that,* she says.

To show I'm unconcerned I aim for flippancy. *The imperatives of modern communication. How did we survive all those years without our mobiles?*

But I've confused her. Her head turns awry so I can see the way her lip is lifted in incomprehension. *What?* Then she realises my mistake. The bottom lip drops. *No, not that. I mean, you know, sorry for calling you a fuddy-duddy earlier.*

Susanna thinks I'm angry with her. The colour in her cheeks is rising and her lips are pursed self-consciously. She tries to make amends. *Listen, when we get into the city how about we have some brunch, huh? What about South Bank? What do you say? I've got a spare hour. I'm meeting a friend later. How're things going with Julia anyway? Last time I spoke to her I got the impression not good.*

The news that Julia is talking about me to someone she hasn't been close to for a long time unsettles me. I feel betrayed once more. And I resent an interloper thinking she has the right to interrogate me about my circumstances. *Julia feels okay talking to you about our private matters, does she?* I can't keep the hurt and anger out of my voice.

Susanna slaps my thigh and chuckles. *Oh, don't be so bloody sensitive, Frank. She's got your interests at heart, old boy, really she has. She mentioned something about you losing your job and getting this crazy idea you're going to write novels or something.* There's an utterance of incredulity straining for release but she manages to swallow it. *I think she reckons you're a wee bit old to embark on a literary career. And I have to say I tend to agree. I think she's hoping it's just a male overreaction and nothing more serious, you know, nothing pathological,* she says instead with a frown, a slow nod and a pout to convey her recognition that the tone of our conversation has shifted. *An injured pride thing. You guys have got pretty fragile egos, most of yous. We could have a talk about it over coffee, huh? It's sort of in my area—you know, psychology.*

For a rash moment I'm convinced the encounter is a set-up, that Julia has somehow anticipated my decision to travel into the city on the train and has contacted her Pilates acquaintance with a psychology degree to intercept and counsel me. *Has she put you up to this?*

Susanna's hands flail at the absurdity of my accusation. *No, no, of course not.*

We're arriving at Macaulay Station. I look past her across the aisle, her belly-laugh and snorting doing nothing to allay my suspicions, and through the window I see my dead friend standing on the opposite platform.

Fuck!

I gape.

The train is still rolling forward and my friend, Charlie, disappears from view, no longer framed by the window. I push past Susanna, alarming her somewhat, probably fearing I'm attacking her for her insolence, but I rush to the other side of the carriage, press my face to the window, inconveniencing a fellow traveller, who protests mutedly and shifts away, unwilling to bear my weight or make a scene.

There's Charlie, back along the platform, staring straight ahead, at nothing, as still as a statue. It's the trench coat he's wearing that convinces me and the fur-lined ushanka cap with a communist star on it that I brought back from China on one of my foreign-correspondence forays, intended as a satirical gift although Charlie never took it that way, sold to me by one of the shyster entrepreneurs on the streets of Shanghai, along with an alarm-clock bearing the chubby face of Mao Tse-Tung between two metal chimes which Julia refused to let me use in our bedroom.

I'm not waking up to look at that tyrant each morning.

It's just a joke. Even the Chinese are sending him up!

Some joke! Millions died under his reign, Frank!

Fuck! Fuck! Fuck! My mind's going haywire. *Excuse me! Excuse me!* I rush to get off. I catch Susanna out of the corner of my eye as I reach the door, as the train comes to a halt. *Sorry*, I call. *Something urgent.*

She stares at me, astonished. *Okay. No brunch?*

I gesticulate to mean what I hope she realises is improbability. She waves me away, amused. *By the way, Frank, what's my name?*

But I'm no longer in a mood to humour her. *No idea*, I mutter. *I'm a psychopath.* She doesn't hear. The doors are sliding closed. *Sandra?* I mouth to her bemused visage in the window as the train begins to move away. In a moment I've forgotten her.

███

My dead friend is standing at the far end of the other platform. I jog along my side until I'm standing opposite him across the tracks. He hasn't performed any vanishing act. His beard has grown longer since last time I saw him in the palliative care unit the night he died.

Charlie?

He stares at me. It's not him!

Relief and disappointment grip me simultaneously. *Hey, where'd you get that coat and cap?* I shout, perhaps aggressively, although my intention is just that he hear me.

He looks along the platform as if he wants a train to arrive to avoid a response. When none materialises he casts his gaze towards the graffiti that covers the walls of a disbanded factory behind me, another spread of indecipherable scribble that covers every available wall and fence the entire length of the railway corridor.

He has exercised his right to remain silent.

He doesn't resemble my friend now that I've had a chance to scrutinize him. The face is gaunt and his lower eyelids sag open, pink and moist. There's a scar breaching the furrows across his forehead. He has the crestfallen look of an underfed bloodhound. The parts of his trousers I can see below the coat are ripped and caked in mud with odd footwear below that, each runner a different colour. I'm glad there's tracks between us because I can guess what he smells like.

Charlie never worried a great deal about his appearance, too engrossed in politics to indulge in minor vanities, but he never looked utterly derelict like the fellow who has somehow acquired his trench coat and ushanka. *They belonged to a friend of mine*. And it occurs to me that Charlie's entire wardrobe was probably left to a local charity, to which this fellow had access.

The man lowers his gaze from the graffiti. *What?* His voice is guttural and hostile. *Yer talking about Charlie?* he says.

But I'm attuned to those sort of tricks. *I called out his name a moment ago. Easy enough to repeat.*

Charlie Johnson?

Astonished he knows the correct surname I peer across the tracks studying him afresh. I've never seen him before. But Charlie had many friends I didn't know, mostly through his political activism. I'm standing beneath a tollway he campaigned against. I'm travelling on the Upfield line whose closure he campaigned against. He campaigned for better public housing. He campaigned for the homeless. As an ex-connie who lost his job to a ticket machine he campaigned for better public transport. In all these campaigns he gathered new friends.

Julia was one of them.

Grass roots campaigns he called them. *That's how you empower people and build the revolution, comrade,* he instructed when I interviewed him about his thesis and back-story for a feature article in our weekend supplement a few months before he died.

After the end of the Cold War he changed his opinion about how soon the revolution was going to happen and how it would be achieved, but he never lost faith in its inevitability. The theory was unequivocal. *Just not in my lifetime,* he told me, knowing he had terminal cancer. And I reminded him the early Christians thought the Second Coming was imminent yet two thousand years later... The implication that Marxism had religious connotations angered him.

I call across the rails, *How do you know Charlie?*

He scratches his whiskers and looks up at the graffiti. *Known him on and off for years. Can't say where I met him exactly. Round here somewhere. He's put me up for a few days when I've needed a break from sleepin' rough. Not this past winter but.* He has a coughing fit and bends while he catches his breath before he continues. *I haven't seen him for a while. Not since he give me this coat a few months ago I think it was, nah, maybe longer.*

I nod and walk around on my side of the station for a moment, casting an eye over the indecipherable graffiti. Typical of Charlie, giving away what he didn't need any longer. *Do you know he died?* I say. *A year ago yesterday.*

My partner in conversation shudders and pulls the coat around him as if an icy gust has swept across the platform. *I thought he might of. He reckoned he had ol' Jimmy Dancer. Well, good luck to 'im. He's better off now, i'n't he?*

No he isn't, I think, peeved at the cliché. I nearly say *what's so good about being dead?* But I take one look at him and think better of it. An answer to that probably differs according to circumstances. Let me be quite unequivocal about this, if it's not obvious to you already, I for one am not looking forward to it.

I had an accident a few years ago when some driver lost control of his car on a wet road and slammed into mine head-on. I remember nothing of it, no pain, not even a vehicle heading towards me. I was thinking about how good it was to get a little rain at last and the next thing I'm aware of is an antiseptic smell and a dreary wall and some uncomfortable tubes in my arm. Three days gone, which could have extended to eternity. That was a dress rehearsal for the end of my life. That's how I learnt there may be no reckoning, no time for a summation of a lifetime's achievements or any chance to recollect treasured moments. Just an infinitesimal transition from banality to nothingness.

A year ago, you say?

Where are you living now? I ask.

Down by the Yarra, opposite the casino. There's a camp.

I know it. Under the elevated line. I walked past there not long ago, saw the swags and blankets and huddled bodies, thinking half of them were probably failed patrons of the establishment across the river. I interviewed three men and a woman. I still have my press ID. I thought maybe Dukakis would accept the story, even though I was only a week retrenched. She loves hard luck stories, especially when there's a villain involved, like a casino, but she declined. When I read the next edition I realised why. A full-page ad featuring the wonderful gambling den.

What are you doing here at Macaulay? I ask.

I jus' wander round Kensington an' Flemington sometimes. Don't get no trouble from no-one round here usually. I did go past Charlie's place as a matter of fact, just for a friendly visit, you know, see how he's goin', an' got no answer. Someone pulled open the curtains for a moment an' looked out. But it wasn't Charlie. I thought he might of been gone or someone was in there looking after him, maybe family, but I don't think he had none. Anyway whoever it was didn't want nothink to do with me.

The bells for the crossing on Macaulay Road begin. The boom gates start to drop. A train approaches his platform.

I'll see ya. Good luck, I shout above the noise before the carriages block my view, expecting him to board. I look for a bench nearby and settle onto it to wait for the next train to the city. The other train continues towards Upfield. I watch it depart. When it's gone, Charlie's ghost is still standing there. I assumed he was heading for Brunswick. There are always derelicts along Sydney Road. We're the only two left at the station. *I thought you'd be catching that one,* I say, speaking into the vacuum the train has left behind.

He shrugs. *What for?*

I throw up my hands in a gesture of incomprehension. *Isn't that why you came to the station?*

He stamps his feet. *I've got all day. It's good to have someone to talk to.*

I give a perfunctory nod, reluctant to spend more time talking to him, now the ghost mystery is solved. I look along the track.

Sounded to me like you wanted to talk, too, about Charlie. He was still stamping his feet, trying to get some blood to the extremities.

No, but I do miss him.

One year ago, you say?

Despite my reluctance I continue to talk about Charlie. *He was a good bloke, wasn't he? An honourable man. Unusual these days, don't you think? Seems to have gone out of fashion. We had our differences but that didn't matter to him. He never took it personally.*

I never rushed to that conclusion either. It had taken me a long time to warm to him. But I observed him for many years. He tried hard to live up to the principles he espoused and largely succeeded, and that seemed a rare quality to me. Nor did I ever see him manipulate others. If I had a criticism to make of him it was that he was indifferent to personal matters. Although he dressed neatly enough and took regular ablutions it didn't bother him that he looked anachronistic in suits he had worn for years, whenever he went out, or the cardigan and zip-up slippers he wore around the house like his father would have worn back in England. His rooms were lost to books and newspapers, flowing off bookcases, over tables and chairs and onto the floor. The kitchen table was impossible to eat at thanks to folders of pamphlets and campaign material. There were no cups without coffee rings and dregs, no wine glasses without tannin stains.

Julia spoke to him now and then about hygiene but he dismissed her concerns with an impatient wave of his hand, as if it were a frivolous concern. Likewise, his health, which he didn't exactly neglect although he often endured pain related to a congenital condition. He occasionally took pain-killers but was suspicious of their effect on his mind, his thinking, his reasoning.

Such stoicism contributed to his demise. He put up with an excruciating pain in his leg without seeking treatment for almost a year, until he was barely able to walk. One day he rang and asked if I'd take him to hospital. In Emergency he had a series of tests, which eventually revealed his cancer, a sarcoma, more than twenty centimetres long growing around his sciatic nerve.

The size of the tumour posed a dilemma for his oncologists, who procrastinated but eventually in a nine-hour operation removed it. The nerve was severed which affected his ability to walk. He needed a walking frame.

He stayed in a rehabilitation ward for a few weeks and then went home, receiving chemotherapy as a day patient. He tried to maintain his routines, struggling to the local shops with his walking frame to buy the newspapers and a few grocery items, which fitted in the frame's basket. He received home help and visits from a community nurse. But insidiously the cancer spread throughout his body. Even so he managed to get himself to Sydney to speak at a conference on Marxism.

After his return I raised the topic of dying. Was he afraid? Had he changed his mind about the possibility of life after death?

I'm nothing but star dust, comrade, he said. *When I die that's it for me. I'm just grateful for the sixty years I've had.*

One evening, two weeks after the Marxist conference, a close friend went around to check on him but he couldn't be roused. She called an ambulance and he was taken to hospital. Within a day he was dead.

I was full of grief and admiration for the way he'd conducted himself. But Julia was furious. He'd neglected his health. *If he'd gone to the doctor when he first got the pain,* she said, *they probably could've treated it and he'd be alive today.*

The ghost of Charlie is watching me. *I've gotta agree with yer. He was a good bloke, our Charlie was. Always supported us.*

Who? The homeless?

The union. I was in the MUA.

You were a wharfie?

Yeah, years ago. We had a big struggle back in the late nineties, against Patricks when they hired thugs to protect them scabs they trained up in Dubai and brought back to smash the union and take all our conditions and pay and everythink. We had a huge picket to stop their trucks gettin' in and out. Lotta community support when they saw them dogs was gonna be used.

I was there, I say, reminiscing. *I'm a journalist. I reported it. Charlie was there too in solidarity. One or two nights.*

Yeah, he told me he'd been there.

Those freezing nights come back to me, standing with hundreds of others, united, singing union songs, arm in arm when it looked like the police were going to break the picket, heroic speeches. I kept to the periphery and during the long lulls, interviewed demonstrators and tried to interview one or two cops, who ignored me. The strike breakers were well out of reach behind wire fences and locked gates with thugs ready for any breach of the perimeters. It looked like the start of something big. The most wildly optimistic picketers mentioned revolution.

The union took the dispute to court and won, I say to Charlie's ghost. *Not much of a victory though. Big compromises.*

He nods and changes his posture. *All them jobs have gone now. Charlie knew I was in the MUA although I didn't know him at the time. He knew I lost me job just like him on them trams, right? That's why he did things for me when he could. You've gotta stick with your comrades, he used to say.*

He lived for a cause greater than himself. A better society. Whether or not he was misguided seems beside the point. The meaning he drew from life encompassed the well-being of others. And that's a rare quality these days.

I hear a train approaching and the boom-gate bells again. It's the next train to the city.

Did you go to his funeral? Charlie's ghost calls out.

Memorial service, I shout as the train sweeps before me. *He left his body to science.*

The sight of Charlie's ghost is blocked until I get onto the train. I forgot to ask his name. Probably wouldn't remember it anyway. In one ear and out the other.

I see him through the window, still standing on the platform. Suddenly the grief that ruined Julia's dinner party returns and tears threaten to embarrass me. From my pocket I fetch a serviette that I kept from last night to blow my nose.

Charlie's ghost pulls the trench-coat collar up and lowers the ushanka earflaps so he looks like a sentinel on the Siberian frontier. Before I lose sight of him he moves towards a bench and settles. Perhaps like Charlie I should have offered him something. Some money. A meal. We could have gone to a nearby café. It wouldn't have been much of an encumbrance. He said it was good to have someone to talk to. It would have been the decent thing to do on my birthday. Something selfless for a change. Perhaps that's what he expected when he delayed catching the train.

It occurs to me, like any ghost he will be there on my return still haunting the platform. I resolve to get off at Macaulay and look for him to see if I can help in any way.

As the train groans towards the city, thoughts of Charlie linger. At this moment he's probably on a slab at Melbourne University being dissected by medical students. I wonder how much is left of him. I imagine bits of him missing where the cancer that had spread throughout his body used to be. They must pop him in a fridge each night to stop him decomposing. They can carve him up for another year or so before they have to cremate what's left.

The thought of it sends a shudder through me. How much longer have I got to live? I'm fifty-five today. How many more years can I count on before oblivion?

I need a distraction.

The apartment towers and giant Ferris wheel at Docklands, the columns of Bolte Bridge come into view, and, once we're through North Melbourne Station and past Docklands Stadium and the city towers, there's a lot more apartments, catering for the new urban lifestyle that many Melbournians and wealthy foreigners have embraced. The suburban dream has become a bit passé. But I would never want to live in one of these concrete boxes no matter what the view, a glimpse of the bay and the hills in the distance and only human madness in between. I like trees around me, and (almost all) birds, at least an allusion to wilderness, to reassure me that reality is not entirely reinforced concrete.

Living in one of these apartments would depress me. But am I happy where I live? Am I happy with my life? Am I content? In a few years I may be nothing, my remains transformed to ash.

Julia! Why does she intrude at this juncture? Is it the model with auburn hair smiling at me from a billboard, reminding me of Julia when she was young? Southern Cross Station with its grey undulating roof and trapped diesel fumes is bustling with regional and interstate visitors as well as urban commuters. I close my eyes and Julia emerges from silhouettes. *Stay away,* I think I hear her say, *leave me alone.* Then she hits me. My eyes spring open. She's gone.

Sorry, says a middle-aged man whose sincerity is concealed by a baseball cap. *Someone bumped me into you. You all right?*

I nod and follow him from the train and out to Spencer Street where he merges and disappears into the crowd. I have no idea what I'm doing—my intention was to get off at Flinders Street—until I realise I'm standing outside The Age building across the road from the station. I've arrived like a moth to lamplight.

For ten minutes I stand before it hoping to catch sight of Dukakis, perhaps heading out to grab a bite, hoping she'd see me and welcome me back. The longer I wait, the more agitated I become. Is she watching from one of the windows above?

There's a cafe nearby with a sign saying 'Free Wi-Fi.' I order a coffee and a muffin, connect my laptop to the internet. I have an urgent email to compose.

2 Chloe

SUBJECT: *Future opportunities*

Dukakis,

How goes it? Busy, busy, busy, no doubt.

Just touching base with a couple of ideas you may be interested in, which I can work on now I'm freelancing.

I was thinking of how you could attract a younger demographic. How would a series looking at ways the new technology is changing everything interest you? The way they communicate, the way they learn, the way they think, what it's doing to their brains, even the way they hook up on dating sites? Are you familiar with these sites? I don't suppose you've ever used them. But I guess the days when journos like us did all our dalliance in the real world are rapidly disappearing.

I'm thinking of calling the series, Millennial Mores, and I want to give The Age first option. It will include an investigation of changing attitudes towards sexuality, and how pornography on the internet is impacting the way couples relate. With the younger staff you've got these days, you're probably aware of this.

I'm wondering too about its impact on the professionalism we used to pride ourselves on. You and I, we were sticklers for maintaining ethical standards at work, never crossed the line, although we came close a couple of times. I remember not too long ago—I hope you don't mind me bringing this up—when you were going through that break-up of your marriage, and you came to work in tears. I don't recall anyone else in our section of the building, just me and you, and you badly needed someone to comfort you, and I kept my distance, even though no-one else was around. My professionalism kicked in and I advised you see a counsellor and you pulled yourself together. But maybe that's a rationalisation. Maybe I was afraid of where any comfort I offered might lead. I can tell you this now because we're no longer colleagues. I just wonder if you and I might have ended up much closer if things had been different.

Can I tell you an interesting story that I once would have turned into copy for you? Something happened to me today, on my birthday, as I was taking the train to the city, which is where I am now, writing this, not far from The Age building, as a matter of fact. I thought I saw the ghost of a dear friend of mine at one of the railway stations. A crusty old atheist like me! Don't laugh. I jumped off the train, I was that sure. It turned out it was a derro dressed in my friend Charlie's distinctive greatcoat and cap. Charlie must have given them to him just before he died.

I had a brief talk to him across the tracks—this was only about half an hour ago—and then I got back on the train and left him there. My head began to swirl with regret, and not just about leaving this poor bloke—I could have at least taken to a cafe and got him something to eat—but all the regrets in my life: like being made redundant, like not being able meet your demands to adapt to the new working conditions, like not warming to the new media quickly enough, like not comforting you when you needed it;. And now I'm pretty sure my marriage is on the rocks. I don't suppose you've heard anything about that on the grapevine, have you? I really regret it. And any minute now I'm going to regret telling you all this, but I need get it off my chest. You've drawn the same short straw I did with you.

Did you ever meet Julia? I think you did, once or twice. I never met your ex-husband. Isn't it weird that we worked together for—how long was it—ten years? I can't say we got to know each other that well, perhaps because I admired you so much as a fellow journalist. But I know nothing else about you. Not even office gossip. But I often think in different circumstances you and I could have hit it off quite well. Maybe in the future our paths may cross again, elsewhere I mean. And I'd look forward to that. But, sorry, I'm right off the track here. This was supposed to be a short message about the Millennial Mores series I'm planning. I know how busy you are. I apologise.

Just one other thing. This derelict was wearing Charlie's cap. It's a ushanka. Ushankas are not often seen in Australia. And here I am right now, wearing a karakul, an Afghan cap, the one I used to wear to work. At home I've got a fez. And I've seen you in some milliner's extravaganza that you'd bought for Cup Day, showing it to the girls at work. Hats. There's a series of articles waiting to be written about them and their cultural significance. I wouldn't mind having a shot at that too, if it had a chance of publication. Do you know Voinovich's novel about Fur Hats? Something in that sort of spirit.

I look forward to hearing from you,

Frank Munro.

3 Madonna

I was intending to go to the State Library to work on my novel, but I change my mind. Instead, after sending the email, I take a tram across the city and a bus to Lygon Street, past the plinth commemorating the Eight Hour Day—eight hours work, eight hours sleep, eight hours play—which stands as a reminder of what used to be, across the street from the stately Victorian era Trades Hall Council building that is slowly declining into ruin.

It's a little after midday and people from the suburbs have arrived for lunch. The Italian restaurants, mainly run these days by new immigrants from Asia and the Middle East, are busy, although most of the waiters still look Italian, probably young foreigners on dubious student visas, gas heaters blasting across the footpath to satisfy customers who enjoy al fresco dining, no matter the weather. I get out at Faraday Street. I want to pay homage to the Carlton Moviehouse, where Julia and I met, a block from Lygon Street, to see what emotions it arouses. It still has its neon light but is boarded up for renewal as retail and office premises, one of its shops pre-leased to an American hamburger chain, New York Minute. And for some reason anger overwhelms me.

When Julia and I were first dating, the Lygon Street precinct was less upmarket, more Bohemian, but when bored denizens of the bland eastern suburbs discovered its coffee houses and quality Italian food, its experimental theatres and student subculture, thanks to its proximity to Melbourne University, its fate was sealed. The gentrification of Carlton accelerated. Rents went up. Prices went up. Everything changed.

The Nova in Lygon Street, a multi-cinema complex with groovy staff, has driven the Carlton Moviehouse out of business. Movie-goers mill around its entrance in an arcade where the cake shop, Brunetti Café, has expanded its business into the premises of a failed book store. It's as popular as the Nova.

I've heard *The Lives of Others* is being reshown in one of the smaller cinemas. I missed it a few years earlier and all my friends, including Julia, have recommended I see it. People are milling around. All these lives I've had nothing to do with. The lives of others. And they know nothing about mine. My life means nothing to them.

My mood couldn't have been more maudlin when, like a portent, I spot Julia sitting at one of the tables outside the café–without her mother or that young PhD student–what's his name? It's this other bloke, this satyr, one of her academic colleagues who was at last night's dinner party, who had been quiet most of the night, the one with the weird wife. He's wearing motorcycle leathers, not the dishevelled suit he had on last night. I try to remember his name. A, B, C–and it comes to me. Cliff Rogerson. How come I remember *his* name? He'd handed Julia a paperback as he was leaving. I wondered what that was about and when I asked her later she was evasive. Maybe that's why I remember his name. Julia's grinning at him and while I stare in amazement she reaches across and squeezes his hand.

Unsure if I should approach I retreat to observe them discreetly. They're laughing, unrestrained laughter, a laughter I've forgotten she's capable of. Her whole body shakes and her hands come up to cover her face as if to capture the pleasure she feels, to hold it like a rare bird. Then she releases it, her hands gesturing joyfully as it flies across the table to Rogerson. Impulsively she stands, moves closer to him and ruffles his hair, laughing, laughing, her belly pressed against his shoulder. Ruffles his fucking hair!

I am bald.

God knows what the joke is.

After a moment she looks around, realising she's attracted the attention of others, who smile or chuckle at her exuberance. Then she glances in my direction as if she senses my presence.

Almost hidden behind a pillar I withdraw rapidly out of sight. Perhaps my whole body isn't concealed but my face is. A few minutes later, when I dare poke my head around again, she's gone.

Rogerson sits alone reading something.

I hasten away across the street into a large bookstore where I browse the new releases, although I don't recognise any of them. My mind is in turmoil. The bookstore is crowded as usual and perhaps I'm spending too much time motionless, obstructing the access of others, because a staff member eventually comes over and asks if she can assist. I stare at her blankly until she steps back as if she has encountered a madman. I shake my head, mumble an apology and leave.

Outside I stare at the window display for a long while, unable to decide what to do. My unique, long-suffering partner, who has given up on me as a lover, has found another. Dear God, Julia—there's not a book on display that can justify my tears, so I move away, my head turned down and away from passers-by.

Two blocks later I turn and hurry back determined to confront them, or Rogerson at least. The café is still crowded but he too has gone. I take the escalator to the Nova foyer where people stand drinking wine or queue to buy ice cream and popcorn or sit waiting for the earlier showing of their movie to end before they can enter their cinema.

There's no sign of Julia or Rogerson. It hardly seems practical to search the complex's sixteen theatres, most of which will be in darkness. At a loss and with no desire to see *The Lives of Others*, or any other movie, I head back to the city on foot to catch the train home.

It's a long desultory walk. An Antarctic wind is gusting north, turned into something capricious and bellicose by the towering concrete labyrinth of the CBD. It chastens Lygon Street. I hug Julia's scarf to my throat but still the wind torments me.

There are moments when I feel like waiting outside the cinema until the two of them emerge two hours hence. I'm sure they'll be together. Would I confront them and demand to know what's going on? Or would I just acknowledge them with a perfunctory greeting as if nothing out of the ordinary was occurring? That way their guilt wouldn't be lost in anger. It would give me the moral high ground. But I know I couldn't pull it off with any aplomb. My nerves are too fragile.

Why Rogerson? I noticed nothing at the dinner party. No secret glances. No moments alone together. Only the gift of a book as Rogerson and his wife departed. What was her name? What was the book? Perhaps I was too focused on the professor—what was his name?—imagining Julia was attracted to him—preposterous now that I think about it—power as an aphrodisiac—that sort of nonsense—while all along it was Rogerson. How have I remembered *his* name? I paid him no attention, except a passing thought that he was arrogant, rakish, even dissolute, with a wife who looked like a battered waif, a typical male academic, in other words. How remiss of me to suspect nothing! Yet I remember his name! Something must have happened at the dinner party for me to tuck his name into my subconscious while other names went missing.

The anguish was grinding away at my vitals. I descend into the City Loop at Melbourne Central and wait on the sterile platform amongst a listless crowd attached to mobile phones.

I haven't checked my phone all morning, have completely forgotten about it. I take it out. A cold dark object, weighty for its size. No messages. Nothing from Julia. Not even a *how's the birthday boy going?* I feel callously forgotten. What will I do when I get home? The house will be as lifeless as a morgue.

When a train arrives I move onto it with the crowd, manage to get a seat opposite two teenagers sharing earplugs and nodding along to their music, looking at each other like they belong to an exclusive society of two.

All through the loop I avoid the eyes of others, looking instead at my window reflection, a lugubrious, middle-aged stranger my only companion, who looks back with the same mystified gaze, until the train emerges from its subterranean gloom near the North Melbourne Station and the image fades to nothing.

The city hunkers under its grey blanket.

I watch a young man board the train, his shaved head emerging from a carapace of tattoos, his arm jerking under the tension of a leash that restrains a fighting dog, propelling him along the aisle as he mutters to himself until he reaches the end of the carriage and turns, averting all heads. I hear someone behind me mutter *menace* bravely.

I return to my unhappy thoughts, trying to imagine Julia alone with Rogerson. What does she find attractive about him? Surely not his clichéd Hollywood looks? That would be too out of character, although in the last few years I've noticed her aesthetic tastes are changing, with sentimentality creeping in where once her judgement was more clinical, sharper, and for an academic surprisingly free of dissimulation. Faces that bore character, the marks of experience, used to gain her attention, not neatly chiselled jaws or alluring mouths and nasal symmetry. That sort of bland perfection irritated her. Not anymore apparently. Perhaps it's his mind. But I got not sense he had one. At the dinner party he spoke less than anyone. Allowed his wife to do the talking. Seemed quite equanimous, in fact. Perhaps that was the attraction.

When I look up, The Menace and his dog have settled on a seat at the end of our carriage. Do I know him? He reminds me of something or someone from past but I can't put a finger on it. We're approaching Macaulay Station beneath the expressway with ramshackle warehouses and abandoned factories on both sides festooned with garish tags behind wire meshing fences.

My gaze settles safely on the graffiti. Lurid incomprehensible script, meaningful only to fellow graffitists. What's the point of it? Some kind of territorial marker like a wild animal pissing along its boundary?

We all need to leave our mark somehow.

I'm thinking how ugly it is and all its ugliness has to do with disenfranchisement and would have ruminated more on the alienated art form but the train stops prematurely across the level crossing with the boom gates down, lights flashing, monotonous cymbals sounding.

Minutes pass. Cars queue.

The passengers sit looking through the windows or at the scrolling text above the door between carriages. *Now arriving at Macaulay Station.* There's no announcement. The line of waiting traffic lengthens, one hundred, two hundred metres of it. Idly I start to count the vehicles. Fifteen, sixteen, seventeen. There are murmurs that dwindle to an expectant silence, broken only when The Menace rises and begins pacing with his dog again, declaring what everyone has already guessed. *Some motherfucker's gone under.* He reaches the end of the aisle and turns. *Why the fuck did he have to jump under my fuckin' train? I gotta get to school.*

He strides back to the door at the end of the carriage, opens it and disappears with his dog into the next carriage, closer to the station.

Shortly afterwards we hear an announcement. *There has been an incident on the track. The train won't be continuing for ninety minutes. Passengers can make their way through the carriages towards the front of the train to disembark onto the platform where it's safe to do so and find an alternative means of transport.*

We follow The Menace, our Pied Piper.

With other passengers I step onto the end of the platform from the second carriage. There's a group of railway staff and onlookers near the front of the train in a conspiratorial huddle. I can hear a siren approaching as I move towards the group.

I try to subdue my urge to see what has happened, an old journalist's habit no doubt and probably morbid. I once saw a man fall from one of those old trams with sliding doors that were often left open. The tram was crossing an intersection while the traffic lights changed to red and an impatient driver of a car accelerated across once the tram had passed. Unaware of the unfortunate fellow lying on the road he ran over him. I watched in horror as the body tumbled beneath the car to be spat out behind, a twisted mess, no longer human. I went home in shock and howled for two hours before writing an evocative article about it, one of my best, for which I won an award. A few seconds was all it took to turn the man into mincemeat.

Here at the station I'm afraid the person on the tracks might be the ghost of comrade Charlie. As I reach the group I hear someone declare the casualty deceased. The voice is trembling. *There was nothing I could do for him.* The speaker is ashen. There are stains on her parka. She might be a nurse.

You did well. One of the railway staff tries to comfort her. *We get one of these every other day somewhere on the network.*

The siren is nearer, louder.

I move towards the nurse. Railway staff put a blanket around her shoulders and hand her something hot to drink.

Excuse me but what's he wearing, the bloke under there? I ask her.

What? She blinks at me incredulously.

Is he in a khaki overcoat? A fur cap?

I don't know. Maybe.

A couple of railway staff in orange jackets move to block my access to her. *Move on, pal. This's not the time.*

I turn and move towards the gap between the platform and the train, needing to see. Again I'm restrained.

There's nothing for you here, pal. The speaker in a railway uniform gripping my arm is hostile, forceful.

I'm a journalist.

I don't care what you are, on your way.

Agitated and disconsolate I traipse with other passengers along a path beside the railway track, northward, in the direction the train had been moving, towards a road serviced by trams. Most of the passengers cross the street to a tram shelter but I need to walk. I'll walk up through the parkland past the zoo to Royal Parade where I can catch a tram to Coburg. My mind is in turmoil. The thought that the ghost of Charlie is under the train distresses me. Dying a year apart. I should have realised his intentions. Maybe I was the last to talk to him. He must have sat for the few hours since I'd last seen him, building up his nerve to jump. I should have offered to help him like my friend Charlie had instead of indulging my own trivial discontents. We could still be in a café somewhere on our third or fourth beer. And here I am, desperate for life to continue, my life at least. It's no cheap thing. It's way too short. A couple of dozen years if I'm lucky and that will be it. The anger is slow in coming at first but then it surges like an avalanche. Just a few minutes earlier, as I was distracted by the industrial ruins along the railway, someone threw his life away and now is mincemeat. I am beside myself with rage.

It has no outlet. I'm not the sort of person who should sprint. Too risky. But sprint I do, holding the karakul in my hand so I don't lose it, my corduroy jacket open, flapping in the air stream. Within a hundred metres I have to stop. I'm gasping for breath but at least the run has tempered the rage and I'm just feeling wasted. It occurs to me that the conversation I had with Charlie's ghost encouraged him to jump.

I stagger on past a mauve building whose sign I notice. *Club Pleasure*. On impulse I digress, straight to its canvas covered entrance and within a few seconds I'm standing at the reception desk, my credit card in the hands of a madam who's suffering the unmistakeable symptoms of ennui.

After charging an amount I can ill-afford she directs me to a room with vinyl armchairs, tasteless paintings of naked women and a screen showing pornography, where I'm to sit and wait for the ladies to enter and introduce themselves. I barely have time to admire the interior decorations when one by one they parade. One way to forget what has shocked you is to subject yourself to a different kind of trauma.

I tell myself this is my birthday present. I tell myself Julia suggested I get a massage and this will be a massage of sorts. They aren't called massage parlours without reason. I'm just paying someone to pamper my body, aren't I? Julia can get a two-hour-long Thai massage and think nothing of it, in fact feel rejuvenated. Why is this any different?

I try to rationalise my presence in a brothel. I could write an article perhaps on the experience and send it to Dukakis, show her I've still got the edge she demanded of my writing. The women greet me and introduce themselves, one or two with well-rehearsed smiles, another looking depressed, another, a Chinese woman, looking desperate, all attired to tantalise me, bras pushing breasts upward, hose and suspender belts. I wilfully ignore the depressed and desperate and choose one called Madonna with a vague resemblance to her namesake—the singer, not the Mother of God—who looks like she might actually enjoy her work, whose crooked smile, mastication and raised chin suggest she may offer something to jam my moral compass.

I follow her along a corridor to a room whose lurid décor reminds me of the cheap hotels Julia and I used to stay in overseas when we were young, except here there's a ceiling mirror. I try to explain to Madonna my heavy breathing is a result of my run and not my presence in the brothel. She instructs me to collect a towel from a small linen cabinet and take a shower.

The water alone is remedial. When I emerge, damp and somehow soft as a baby, my breathing back to its wheezy normality, she gestures toward the bed. *You wanna take my clothes off?* she asks, still chewing gum.

No, no. It's okay. My jaded nerves sent the words an octave too high. *You do it.*

She slips out of her underwear nonchalantly and moves onto the bed without paying me much attention. Her breasts are small and her pubic hair is missing. Just outside is Macaulay Station with mincemeat all over the tracks.

You're limp. What's up? She reaches past me to get a condom from a bowl on the side table. She takes my dick and begins to rub and tug it while she tears the packaging with her teeth.

Flesh and death.

To my shame I'm erect soon enough.

That's better.

Before she applies the condom she inspects my appendage, I assume for any sign of contagion. Then deftly using her mouth and fingers she rolls it on and mounts me, done with such efficiency even the time and motion people would have trouble recommending improvements. I last less than thirty seconds. I groan and turn my head away, embarrassed. There isn't even the consolation of pleasure.

That wasn't much. She almost sounds disappointed.

I haven't done it for a while.

How do you extract so much mincemeat from beneath a train?

She climbs off.

What happens now? I ask, having paid for half an hour.

It takes her a moment to think of something. *You can scratch my back if you like.* She sits on the edge of the bed. I do what I'm told. *Ouch! Gently. You have no idea, have you?* I stop. Tiny red welts have appeared on her skin. She gets up and stands before the mirror to inspect the damage. *What's wrong with you? Bloody hell!*

Sorry.

You can take another shower before you leave if you need to. She signals with her head the location of the shower as if I had forgotten where I was a few minutes ago.

How about we shower together? I sound desperate.

Her head tilts and in the moment before she begins chewing again gives a cynical smile. She points at the spent condom which is about to slip off my dick.

I remove and hold the protector up helplessly until she takes it and deftly ties a knot to prevent the contents spilling. She tosses it into a tiny bin whose lid she opens with a foot lever. *Use the same towel,* she instructs as she begins to straighten the bedding.

I feel hysteria creeping up on me again. *You couldn't do a song for me, could you, Madonna? A rendition of* Like a Virgin, *perhaps?*

Get outa here.

I'll skip the shower.

Yeah, whatever.

Ablutions to remove traces of the sexual encounter are the least of my concerns. There's hardly a need to conceal my activity, no suspicious wife at home waiting. Nevertheless, outside when I hasten away, I pull my jacket collar up, hold it around my face, my nose catching the sour scent of Julia's scarf.

Soon I'm walking through the parklands feeling disgusted with myself, morally traumatised, past the site where Burke and Wills began their fateful journey into the wilderness, which seems worth reflecting upon, given my circumstances.

Happy birthday, Frank! What a present you've given yourself! Another fucking year gone. Another step closer to the grave and what have you achieved? Fucking nothing. Just shame and disgust. Any wonder Julia is out rooting other men. Who knows how many? Maybe the entire Department. You can't blame her for that. Maybe you should do the honourable thing and offer to leave, offer her a divorce—ah, not necessary—not married. My own trek into the wilderness.

When I arrive home a pall of silence hangs over the place. The house is cold. Icy. I go straight to the switch for the ducted heating. The silence is dreadful. I've never felt so alone. Turn on the tellie. Oprah. That's good. Lots of animated discussion. Laughter. Applause. A glass of wine. That would help. No, a bottle. Of red. Or two. Cleanskins. Something caustic. Julia doesn't like the cheap stuff. But I do. I appreciate the rasp as it slides down my throat. Cocooned in my old armchair I want to forget Madonna. And Julia. And the ghost of Charlie. Mincemeat. I want to cry. I whimper. And guzzle wine. And argue with Oprah. Who has such poor taste in literature! Such predictable sentimental shit! Turn up the volume. Argue. The room's warm. Cosy. I sob. I blubber. I pass out. When I come to, it's dark. Oprah is finished. Some other nonsense about home renovations is in her place. I call out Julia's name. No answer. Hungry, I stumble to the kitchen and find some leftovers from the dinner party in the fridge, some hors d'oeuvres and slices of smoked salmon, which I take back to the lounge to eat while I watch two couples enthusiastically demolish their houses. I eat and drink and choose the couple I hate more. I curse and abuse them. *Fuckwits! Imbeciles! Fools! Clowns! Have you no fuckin' self-respect?* Later I pass out again.

I must have.

It's morning. My birthday over. Fifty-five and one day but who's counting? My shirt is sodden from spilt wine. I wander the house, return to the bedroom twice, unable to believe it's unoccupied. No Julia. I shout her name. But it's the wattlebird that answers. Damn fucking bird! I've never hated anything so much. Where's the hose? Out the front door. Along the path. The tap. Turn it on. Full bore. Rush towards the tree. *Where are you, you fucker? Time for a bird bath. How come you don't squawk when I come near you, you fucker?* Squirt the hose indiscriminately. A fireman inside an inferno.

A voice. *You* are *mad!* Not the doctor, surely? *Genuinely fucking mad!*

Yes! Fuck! Gaping at me. This time in a raincoat.

What do you want? I cry.

He has his iPhone ready, videoing me lest I turn the hose on him again. Instead I turn it on myself, hold it above my head and give myself a drenching. The icy water snatches my breath and twists it into a whoop and howl. My flab begins to bounce and recoil. *Oh, God, this is salubrious!* I shout. *You should try it someday, Doc.*

But the doctor, bless him, is backing away, his phone pointed at me. This time he'll have a video record. I toss the hose aside, the trigger locked on, leaving it to swish and jerk dementedly around the garden.

Inside I drip my way along the passage and return to the arm-chair. I think about Julia. Where is she? I vaguely remember her saying she might stay over at her mother's but I sit shivering in my sodden clothes, imagining her curled up with a guy I'm no match for. Where's my mobile? I search my pockets. No need for that new trick I recently learnt of ringing my own number. I find it safely dry in my jacket, which I must have taken off after I arrived home. I find her number and press. Straight to the voice bank. I hang up. She will know I've rung but didn't leave a message. I call her mother.

Frank? Do you know what hour it is?

I look at my phone. *Eight twenty-seven.*

I feel her exasperation.

It's early Sunday morning, Frank. This better be important. I was having a nice dream.

My teeth are chattering. I should have dried and changed. *Could I speak to Julia, please?*

Another wave of exasperation accompanied by a groan this time. *What's wrong with you? You sound sick.* She can hear my dental percussion, which sounds like a jazz improvisation. *Have you tried her mobile?*

More gnashing. *She's not answering.*

Well, what do you expect at this time of day?

Is she there? No answer. *If she is, could you go and ask her to come to the phone, please, Aggie?*

Silence. An old woman's collusive mind edging through a sleepy fog. *No, I can't. Ring her later.*

It's urgent.

Nothing's that urgent. Go see a doctor, Frank, and stop bothering me. She hangs up.

So she's in on this, up to her eyeballs in deceit, covering for her adulterous daughter. When it comes to justice–doing the right thing–honesty–family loyalties always take precedence.

Julia's obviously not in her childhood bed. She's curved into the crescent flesh of her lover elsewhere. A hotel room maybe. Spooning it. I imagine his huge flaccid cock resting, sated, in the crevice of her buttocks.

Red wine is the only way to deal with an image like that. There's another bottle by my chair. Thank God it has a screw top and not a cork. *Julia, darling, sweetheart, you should be home with me,* I wail. *I need you today, more than ever. Someone who knew Charlie was killed yesterday. He went under the train I was on.* I send this message through the ether.

I believe we sometimes communicate telepathically. There were too many coincidences for it not to be true. I remember the time when I was at the State Library, researching something or other, when I felt she was in the building and I went searching for her and found her in the reading room. She wasn't surprised. After that we often met in the library, sometimes planned, sometimes spontaneously. It became our refuge.

There were many other times. Many others.

If she gets the message this time, the bit about Charlie should do the trick. She shared the grief.

I'm drinking from the bottle which is already half empty. I ring her mobile again. No answer. I text. *Did you get my message?* My teeth are sounding like cymbals on the lip of the bottle. Fuck, I need to write. I need to write something. It's the only way to stay sane. I place the bottle on a side table and heave myself out of the armchair. A hot shower is necessary to stop this chattering of teeth. Oh, elixir! Hot water! I stand for half an hour beneath it, well, not actually stand, for my legs rebel, I sit most of the time on the tiles, my balls against the drain grate. By the time I get to my study, dried and powdered, in my bathrobe and fluffy slippers, I'm ready to pour my heart out, honestly, openly, a testament to love.

My love. Which I know I'm losing.

4 Cliff

Swimming into deep water

Julia met Cliff Rogerson at a critical moment in her life. At home her relationship to Frank was gradually expiring. Or she felt it was. There was nothing specific. They certainly didn't fight or argue, except over trivial matters that were really manifestations of unspoken discontent and boredom. Lost somewhere in the years of living together was the enchantment she used to feel in their intimate moments or sometimes when she watched him from a distance as he went about his daily activities, his mindfulness of their shared space, his kindness and tolerance towards people she could barely abide, the grace he had with animals, his forbearance with demanding children, knowing he wanted his own more than she did. There was still some affection, some warmth, but it was from embers. After a fire only charred wood and ashes remain.

She was lecturing and tutoring Women's Studies in the School of Humanities after completing a PhD in Media and Communication (Cinematic Studies). Cliff Rogerson was a new addition to the faculty, a craggy-faced, dark-eyed sociologist who caught her attention with an hilarious parody of the recently deposed Prime Minister, at one of Professor George Petrus's weekend retreats.

It occurred to her that she hadn't laughed so robustly since the student revues she used to attend as an undergraduate years earlier. Her laughter took her by surprise. She wasn't prepared for the wonderful release of tension, despite one of Rogerson's jokes being at the expense of a woman, the ex-Prime Minister's imperious chief of staff. It could well have been construed as sexist but laughter impaired her critical faculty. She was more relaxed than she had been in months—years, maybe.

Rogerson had noticed her laughter and asked George Petrus for an introduction. The professor obliged with a guiding hand in the small of Julia's back, one eyebrow raised and an ironic warning about fraternizing with charismatic men, before tactfully finding an excuse to move away.

She was flattered by the attention and charmed by Rogerson's wit. Her favourite TV period dramas had protagonists like him. Always they were charming with an air of mystery, of earlier tragedy. They had fortitude and a capacity for reckless passion. Managing an ironic smile at her own impressionability, she accompanied him onto a broad patio overlooking the resort's golf course, where they sat at a hand-hewn blackwood table drinking cocktails until she could barely remember where she was and what she was doing, or even who she was with.

'Feel like playing?' Cliff Rogerson said when his repartee began to wane and was in danger of putting her to sleep.

'What?' she uttered, startled.

Pleased with her reaction he delayed a response to allow her to imagine the possibilities. 'Golf,' he said with a slight gesture towards the links.

'Golf?' For a moment the meaning of the word eluded her. She frowned and blinked in a muddle. 'I've never played that. It's never even crossed my mind.'

'I've never played either but it might be fun. Take out our frustrations on a wee white ball.'

Her breathing felt constricted. 'I'd prefer a walk along the beach.'

'Ah, now you're talking.'

He took her hand and pulled her out of her comfort zone. An ambivalent grip. Surprisingly soft but resolute. Her will deserted her.

'So what are your frustrations?' he asked, leading her along a sandy path through melaleucas.

'I didn't say I had any.' She tried to focus through her pleasant fugue. 'Did I?'

He tugged her along at a pace that alarmed her legs. No bloke had ever dragged her around like this that she could remember, certainly not Frank who would have considered it atavistic and demeaning. Normally she, too, would have demurred but in her present state she found it amusing.

When he grinned she noticed nicotine-stained canines and got the giggles, thinking of the silly vampire movies she liked.

'I bet you have,' he protested, allowing his voice to rise in mock disbelief. 'How long did you say you've been married? Nearly twenty years?'

'I never told you I was married.'

'Yes, you did, after your fourth daiquiri.'

'How many?'

'Four and that wasn't your last either.'

She pulled on his hand until she was clinging to his arm. 'God, I don't normally drink that much. I haven't been drunk in years. Did I tell you who I was married to?'

'I think you said Frank. "Frank by name. Frank by nature," is how you put it. Nice guy, apparently. Perhaps too nice for your liking. Twenty years and no children.'

'What about you? You married?'

'I told you that too. Married with kids. The requisite two point five.'

She laughed or snorted, the sound she made recoiling, intriguing her, unlike any noise she had ever made. 'You can't have point five of a child. Point five!'

'Let's not go there.' He sounded earnest for a change. 'Come on, frustrations. You tell me yours and I'll tell you mine.'

'You go first.'

The melaleucas were thinning, providing space for sharp coastal grasses, their astringent scent succumbing to brackish air. She could hear the ocean, the rhythmic crashing, the sucking retreat. She felt perfectly content clinging to the arm of a virtual stranger.

They stumbled down a sand hill together, hooting and guffawing. When they reached the beach he turned and grabbed both her arms, holding them against her torso as effectively as a straitjacket. 'You're my frustration.' He studied her wildly, muttering words of delight, from which she decrypted *beautiful* and *sexy* and *want* and *fuck*.

When he tried to kiss her she turned her head away, and with a strength that surprised him, broke free of his grip. 'Don't force me, Cliff,' she warned. 'I've had some bad experiences with men.'

'How many?'

'Oh, fuck, what sort of question is that?'

'I'm curious. I wondered if you'd been unfaithful.'

'This was before Frank.'

He held her shoulders and stared at her. 'What, you've never had a bit on the side since then?'

She looked away and shook her head, like a child who had thought she had done something wrong.

'That's unnatural,' he said and laughed.

She removed his hands from her shoulders and took a few steps towards the ocean. 'Let's just enjoy the sea for a moment, for a while. This is happening too fast for me. I'm drunk, Cliff.'

He hesitated, mindful of the repercussions, nodded and dropped onto the sand. 'Come on, we'll just sit.' He leant on an elbow and watched the waves.

She flopped down beside him with a grunt, onto her bum, her legs waving.

'Oh, Julia, that was graceful.'

She snorted to repress an adolescent giggle. 'I'm a demure sort of gal.' She released the declaration through an opening at one end of her mouth.

They sat looking at the sea while their merriment subsided and their breathing steadied. Seagulls hovered and glided above the waves. With her mouth open Julia could taste the salt air. She was pleased that the air was cold.

'I've always loved the sea down this way,' Cliff said, moving his head to look at her. 'It's the Southern Ocean, straight off the Antarctic. Untamed, icy cold water, barely damaged by our excesses.'

His earnestness partially sobered her. She nodded and looked anew towards the sea. 'I love it too,' she said ruefully in the face of its indifference. 'It gives me a perspective I often lack.'

'And what would that be?'

For a moment he thought she wasn't going to answer, but she was searching for elusive words. 'It's a reminder that I know so little about the world, the universe,' she said, 'and that my place in it is so tiny.'

She allowed her shoulder to press against his.

They sat unspeaking for a while, enjoying the afternoon. Julia twice glanced slyly at his supine body with its classical proportions, its latent power and athleticism. The tranquillity of the beach and the fermented warmth in her entrails were affecting her emotions. She lay on the sand beside him, closed her eyes and amused herself imagining a life together.

His voice intruded into her reverie and she lifted her head to squint at him through the descending sunlight. 'I've an idea you might like,' he said. 'How about we take a dip in the sea? There's no one around. Sober us up a bit and then we can head back. I'm sure the Prof has some cerebral dessert ready for us.'

If Frank had been with her and made the suggestion she would have refused and called him crazy, but it seemed the perfect way to end the afternoon with Rogerson. 'Okay. You go first.'

Despite the cold, Rogerson stripped off his clothes and walked into the surf. As she undressed more hesitantly she stole glances at his body. His beauty aroused her. He was far more virile than Frank. She felt her breath quicken but her conscience still kept a tight rein on her impulses.

Up to his thighs he turned to face her as she approached the water's edge. His grin and the stirring of his dick from its dark nest made her self-conscious. She tried to steady herself as she entered the sea but unbalanced at the first wave and toppled sideways.

She shrieked as the icy water washed over her. She felt his hands lifting her, heard his laughter, felt his hands move across her wet breasts, heard him utter, 'You're fucking beautiful.'

Her mind was churning like the breakers. Then his dick was in her grasp. He groaned as she began to squeeze it. She managed a semblance of control, moved to a position behind him, pressed her belly against his buttocks and pumped him until his torso, facing seaward, heaved and convulsed. His semen fell into the waves.

As he bent forward, catching his breath, she plunged away and swam into deeper water beyond the breakers to be alone. She had crossed a boundary and now there was only open ocean. She could keep swimming but knew she would eventually drown somewhere beyond the sight of land.

The ruse

Back at the resort they separated and socialised with different people, until Professor Petrus summoned his colleagues for a discourse with aperitifs on the documentary as a tool for social research.

'Not my area,' he confessed, 'but I like to keep an open mind and since we have some experts here with us—.'

Julia spoke about the need for the documentary maker to be in the documentary itself. 'The visible narrator,' she called it. 'All documentaries are subjective. Why not be upfront about it? You are part of the narrative. It's unavoidable. It's all about being honest with your audience.'

'How about respecting their intelligence then?' Cliff Rogerson interjected. 'I've always found "the visible narrator" as you called him—'

'Her.'

'—her—a distraction, often an annoying distraction, which is usually a tactic for obscuring a weak argument, a weak case, a weak narrative. There's so many wannabes, so many aspiring David Attenboroughs or Louis Therouxs or Mike Moores out there, most of them forgettable. But even more forgettable is what their damn documentaries are about. Some jerk wants to get women's opinions on what's wrong with his willy (sniggers from the assembled academics), another why he's a premature ejaculator, another why she had a boob job, another why she prefers sex with dildos (more sniggers, some chuckles). The list is endless. Sex, sex, sex. And egos, bloody inflated egos.'

He received murmurs of support.

'I'm not referring to these tabloid documentaries,' Julia attempted a defence.

'What then?'

'I don't know, there's lots. And some of them *are* about sex. They don't all have to be prurient. I'm referring to serious research documentaries that accompany proper scientific field work.'

'For example?'

'For example–since your focus seems to be on the erogenous zone (general laughter)–some documentaries about female genitals have been valuable for women where research indicates the majority are quite anxious about their own–oh, God–seeing the variety–you know, realising you're not some kind of freak. That sort of documentary is quite affirming.'

'Really? Affirming?'

The subdued laughter around the room shamed her.

'Maybe it's a feminist thing,' she said quietly, more to herself than to others, aware her ability to articulate had deserted her.

'Don't get me wrong, I'm as much a feminist as the next bloke,' Rogerson responded with his charming grin. 'I respect women's rights. I'm all for equality. But we should try to minimise the subjectivity thing that's creeping into the medium. And, I regret to say, it could well be a feminist influence.'

'This is a bit tangential,' interceded Petrus, concerned the discussion was heading into hostile territory and feeling protective of Julia whom he considered his protégé. 'Who else has something to say?'

Julia looked across at Rogerson, sitting diametrically opposite her smiling, as if he'd enjoyed their public spat, while the discourse was taken elsewhere by others.

After dinner she left the group on the pretext of weariness in order to avoid further interaction with Rogerson. She returned to her cabin, her mind in turmoil. She could hardly believe what she'd done in the surf. Stricken with guilt, she couldn't stop thinking of Frank and then was furious with herself that such patriarchal mores could surface, relics of her upbringing. In defiance she felt she should set aside her guilt and have a fully-fledged affair, a brief one, but then couldn't escape the thought that it would hurt Frank if he ever found out. It was important to her to avoid being deliberately cruel to anyone, especially the people she loved or who loved her.

Then there was Rogerson's unexpected intellectual challenge, which made her look obtuse. He must have known after what had happened at the beach that her mind would be unprepared for such an onslaught. There lay cruelty. What sort of game was he playing? Why was he toying with her? Was it convoluted revenge for not succumbing completely at the beach?

But her thoughts suddenly gave way to exhilaration and panic when, shortly after midnight, she heard a soft knock on her door.

Cliff Rogerson arrived in a silk robe and slippers with a bottle of champagne under his arm. 'I noticed your light was still on,' he whispered when she opened the door. 'Can't sleep?'

'What do you want?' she said, already knowing the answer, stepping aside to allow him to enter, unable to resist checking outside to see if anyone had noticed. But the stillness and silence was only broken by the melancholy call of a mopoke.

He looked askance at her and chuckled. 'Whatever's on offer. Companionship, sex, further discussion of the role of feminism in a post-modern world. It's your call.'

He dropped into a chair and crudely threw his leg over its armrest, his thigh flesh exposed, bottle dangling from his hand.

'You're still drunk.' Her voice was subdued.

'Making the most of this scholarly occasion.'

'What was that all about, before dinner?' she demanded, making sure her door was locked. 'You attacking me like that?'

'It was all subterfuge, my darling,' he said with a sanguine sigh, the bottle waving casually. 'So that none of those present would suspect we were lovers.'

'We're not lovers,' she responded dully as she moved to the bed where she propped cross-legged in a winter nightie. 'A bit of foolish, drunken hanky-panky does not an affair make.'

'I doubt your husband would agree.'

'Frank's not going to know. Would you tell your wife?'

'If he's not going to know why not make the most of it? Placate the frustrations.' He raised the bottle as a peace offering. 'Drink?'

She closed her eyes and hesitated. 'It's not that simple, Cliff.'

'It's as simple as you want to make it.'

'I don't even know who you are.'

'Does it matter?'

'It matters to me.'

Rogerson shrugged as he swung his leg off the armrest.

She caught sight of his penis and her chest constricted.

'Any flutes?' He stood at the end of the bed and struggled with the cork.

'There are glasses in that cupboard,' she managed to say.

'Shall I give you a bio? Would that help?'

'You've got a caustic sense of humour, I've learnt that much.'

'Ah, but I'm a sensitive guy.'

He removed two tumblers from the cupboard, poured the champagne and took one across to her. 'Here's to pleasant extra-curricular activities.'

He clinked her glass and took a swig before lowering himself onto the edge of the bed. 'Sweet Julia, you look so gorgeous. I wished I'd found you years ago.'

She held both her hands forward, one with the glass. 'No, no, no, no, no,' she pleaded. 'Please, Cliff. The easiest thing in the world for me would be to "let you have your way with me". God knows I could do with it. But I can't let it happen. Not at the moment. Not yet.'

'Not yet? That sounds promising. All right, it's the bio then.' He looked around the room at the prosaic décor. 'I was born in Melbourne on the eleventh of November, nineteen seventy-five, the day of Gough Whitlam's dismissal, a breech birth apparently for which my mother, bless her soul, never forgave me, or Whitlam for that matter, who she blamed for every upheaval, political, spiritual, emotional and gynaeco-logical that occurred that day and thereafter. My father was too overtaken by the "coup", as he called it, to concern him-self with her contractions or my birth. An unfortunate start and sadly the pinnacle of our father-son thing. Yes, things went downhill from that moment onwards. No matter. I'm inclined to agree with Henry Miller on difficult births at least. Have you ever read him? Fascinating reading for a feminist. Like throwing dynamite into the flames of righteous indigna-tion. But evocative prose, evocative prose. He said something like this: "They had a hell of a time getting me out of the womb. Why leave a cosy place where everything is warm and gratis?" It's never the same after you're born. My father wanted to call me Gough but my mother refused. She was outraged. Cliff Richards was her favourite singer. Although my father wasn't a fan, he didn't object. He thought the country had gone over a cliff.'

Julia reached over and gripped his forearm. 'Cliff, there's no need. I never meant—'

'No, no, it's fine, now I've started.' His smile was exaggerated.

'No, stop it.' She put her glass on the side table and combed her fingers through her hair. 'Just listen. Please. You're a very attractive bloke, right? I find you very attractive. And I enjoyed what we did today but that's as far as it's going. My marriage means a lot to me despite the state it's in at the moment. You've met me at a vulnerable time. I don't know how things are between you and your wife, but Frank and I, well, this slow dissolution is killing me. The time may come, soon, when I decide I'm leaving him. But he's a darling. It's really hard.'

His smile was a private affair.

He leant forward, drew her head towards him and kissed her forehead. 'You're being very kind to him but not so considerate of your own needs.'

Moving back to the armchair and sitting more modestly, he took a lingering draught of champagne. The moments that followed were awkward.

Julia knew Frank would be distraught if he found out about this scene but he wouldn't rage and rant. She wished he would. His acceptance of matters that adversely affected him without a demonstrative moment of dismay, much less anger, much less fury, was part of the reason the ardour had vanished from her feelings for him. She suspected he had trained himself into passivity to avoid any accusation of bad masculine behaviour, his fear of being labelled sexist or macho. The thing about this other man in her room was his confidence, his virility, his ego, which seemed unassailable, which promised excitement, passion, possibilities, all which were much diminished or gone from her life.

She couldn't blame him for intruding in the middle of the night, expecting sex. Having masturbated him earlier in the day, there was a certain logic to it. She hated the term *cock-teaser* but that's what she felt like, even if she'd gone a step beyond that. She imagined, despite his tolerance, that's what he was thinking. The confusion he provoked was preventing her acting decisively.

She should have demanded he leave and let her sleep. Instead she lay back and drew up her nightie. 'Here's what you want,' she said in a voice that betrayed her anxiety. 'Get it over with.'

He stood, placed his glass on a bench and considered what she was offering. Another private smile. He moved to the bed, sat on its edge and placed a hand upon her pubic hair. It might have been a stone dropping into a pond. When the ripple reached her throat a sound emerged. Regret. Pleasure. Guilt. Pleasure. He leant forward and kissed her softly.

'Sweet Julia,' he whispered. 'Until you've worked out what you really want, this is not going any further. You've got to want it as much as me or it'll be a disaster. Just sleep on it. I'll see you at breakfast.'

His hand lingered for a moment and gently squeezed.

Another ripple. A larger stone.

The emptiness when he moved away was her vision of the future.

She listened to his footsteps retreat along the path until she was left with the intermittent sound of a mopoke somewhere in the darkness.

Nothing else.

She stared at the ceiling, quite stunned.

Respect was the last thing she had expected at that moment. Her gratitude was boundless. Again she felt regret. Same instance. Different focus. She placed her own hand over her vulva and squeezed, trying to recapture the sensation. But what she experienced was abandonment. It had one explanation, which made her panic. *Fuck, fuck, fuck, fuck! I don't want to fall in love with someone else. Poor Frank, I'm losing you.*

What was there to lose?

She almost cried remembering the lengths Frank had gone to for a date. Those months of following her to the cinema, his autodidactic crash-course in cinematography to impress her, the gaffes he made trying to be an expert, his dismay, his desperation when he realised his errors. His endeavours to get her to think highly of him succeeded but not for the reasons he imagined. It was his failure to desist in the face of humiliation, and his self-deprecation, his honesty. He never got angry when she laughed at him, accepting her criticism earnestly. Unlike most men she knew he never condescended. She grew fond of him but didn't fall in love with him. They dated. They fucked. They went to special places, like Paradise Falls near the Wombat Ranges, sat against its majestic concave wall behind the gentle cascade, with a view down the deserted valley, and agreed it felt like a sacred place. They ended up living together. The future didn't come into their calculations until one day something quite banal happened that changed everything.

They were waiting in a bus shelter one overcast day with flurries of cold rain curling around its edges, the bus still ten minutes away. They huddled together for warmth with Frank's coat wrapped around their shoulders.

Julia saw them first, a couple approaching with a dog on a leash, neither dressed for the cold, torn T-shirts and jeans, thongs on their feet, filthy, matted hair. They were arguing, the woman gesticulating wildly, the man sullen, the dog, a thick-set, brindled, steely-jawed beast, pulling him forward. As they passed the shelter, the man stopped and asked Frank for a cigarette. The woman kept walking, shouting at the man to 'fuckin' hurry, fuckin' stop wastin' fuckin' time.' She turned momentarily, swaying, abusing him, while he strained against the indomitable dog.

'Keep yer fuckin' mouth shut!' he shouted back at her.

'I don't have any,' Frank said with a nervous smile.

'What about yer bitch? She got any?'

Julia ignored him. She looked along the street hoping for a bus.

'Fuck yers then.'

The dog pulled him sideways and he screamed at it.

'She's not a "bitch",' Frank said calmly. "She's a woman."

The man yanked the leash hard enough for the dog to lose its balance. When it stumbled he dragged it back on its side. With wild eyes it managed to get to its feet, growling.

'What the fuck did you say?'

Julia grasped Frank's arm. 'Leave it, Frank.'

'Come on, Corrie!' the woman shouted, her impatience with the temperature evident in her stamping feet. 'The ol' girl'll have fags. Let's just get there. It's fuckin' freezin'.'

Corrie hesitated, his desire for a cigarette or warmth conflicted with his desire to confront Frank. His eyes bulged and his jaw moved sideways. He decided spitting at Frank's face was a fair way to settle the dispute.

He had no phlegm and little saliva. So what Frank felt was a vapid spray across his cheek and forehead. An impotent assault. Embarrassed, Corrie turned and strutted away, led by the dog.

But the dog went one way around a sign pole and Corrie went the other without realising it, until he stumbled and cracked his head against the metal.

He screamed at the dog, yanked it back against the pole and began to kick its belly. The dog howled and cowed. But Corrie wasn't satisfied. He caught sight of a beer bottle in the gutter and decided to use it as a cudgel.

He brought it down hard on the dog's head with a sickening thud.

Frank sprang to his feet and approached. 'Leave off, you idiot! The dog's done nothing wrong.'

Corrie stopped, unable to believe the intervention. He gaped at Frank. 'You got a problem, cunt?'

'Your cruelty's the problem, man.' He took out his phone and waved it in the air. 'Leave the dog alone or I'll call the RACV.'

He meant to say the RSPCA but in the stress of the moment he confused his abbreviations. Corrie didn't notice but Julia did. She would tell her friends about it later as comic relief in her dramatic recount of his courage, which landed him in hospital with a fractured skull and stomach wound. But she would never tell anyone it was the moment she fell in love with him because it sounded absurd even to her own ears.

She heard a dog bark into the night as she lay awake in her cabin, an aggressive challenge for someone or something to reveal itself. It lasted no more than a minute. Then silence descended again.

Was Cliff awake? Was he thinking of her? What would he make of her if she revealed how she had fallen for Frank? He would laugh aloud, surely.

Why the hesitation?

After Frank was discharged from hospital, she hardly left his side for six weeks, dealing with his recovery. His assailant had bashed him with the bottle and then smashed it against the concrete gutter to use its sharp edge as a dagger. When the assailant saw blood he fled, dragging away his injured dog by its leash. Julia kept the stomach wound clean, bathing it several times a day with disinfectant. The wound healed leaving a crooked scar which she considered a symbol of all that was good about Frank.

As a child Julia had been allowed to keep pets. Dogs and cats. Her favourite had been Thistle, an untidy terrier. She took him for walks in the streets of her neighbourhood and some-times along a track through the bush around a littered creek where he chased rabbits and endeavoured to roll in any excrement he could find. After each walk she brushed him, trying to tame his coat, or washed him down with a hose. The end of the grooming was marked with a kiss and a hug and squeals of approval. Thistle reciprocated with licks and a vigorous squirm, bursting out of the embrace to accelerate around the yard in a fit of liberation. Each night she took him to his kennel, fussed over his bedding, tucked him in for the night and reminded him to be a good boy and not cause any trouble while she slept.

She loved him but he had some annoying habits. He dug holes under fences and attacked other people's pets, and whenever he was left alone during the day he bothered the neighbourhood with his constant barking.

When her father, a bank manager who worried about his reputation in the community, had the dog euthanized, her mind slipped a cog and never recovered. She would never forgive him nor anyone else in her family for their indiffer-ence, nor herself for allowing it to happen.

From the dark resort room she remembered how that terrible incident had ruined her childhood. She wished Cliff had stayed to talk. She might have told him what had happened next and hopefully it would help him understand her indecisiveness.

People had commented on the change in her personality. Gone was the spontaneous, garrulous child. She grew up sullen and introverted. Throughout her high school years she wanted no close friends and had none, which left her vulnerable to bullies. They tormented her constantly about her appearance, calling her an 'anorexic bitch' and mocking her scholarly diligence. The bullies were mainly other female students who could see her erotic potential and wanted to do as much damage as possible before she reached it.

When she was fourteen there was a group of four girls in her class who lured her into a park with the promise of sharing some dope. Instead, at a prearranged gathering, they held her down and removed her panties and charged their male companions five dollars each to look. It precipitated her first suicide attempt in her father's shed where she tried to hang herself with some old rope she attached to a rafter. Before she was strangled it snapped. Shocked and shamed, her family put her in a psychiatric hospital for six months and then onto antidepressants, which she used throughout her time at high school.

While she was in the hospital, she had sex for the first time, with a psychopath two years her junior. It was the start of a period she later called her 'years of promiscuity'. She began to fuck boys and men of all ages in all sorts of places. She went on the pill. But so much sex had a devastating effect on her emotions, this constant need to have her body plundered as a way of declaring *you can't touch me.* By the time she graduated from high school she hated men.

She sought solace in the virtual world of cinema and literature. When she had finished her schooling and was accepted into university, she cut all ties to her family, renting a room in a shared student house, but largely keeping to herself. Nevertheless, the males of the household enjoyed nocturnal visits to her room and there was anonymous sex at the club she went to every Saturday night.

Her second suicide attempt occurred in her first undergraduate year. She took an overdose of pills and again was lucky enough to be found by Susanna, one of the co-tenants, a sweet young woman who liked her despite her antisocial tendencies, who did the uncool thing of calling an ambulance.

In hospital Julia had her stomach pumped.

Her housemates never assumed her actions were suicidal. They figured she had just accidently overdosed, which could have happened to any one of them since there seemed to be an endless pharmaceutical supply around the house.

When she returned she stopped having any form of sex, even masturbation.

The day Julia left hospital, Susanna, the housemate who had called the ambulance, came to her room to see how she was doing. They talked for a while with Susanna trying to keep the conversation as cheerful as possible. At one point she mentioned a women's consciousness-raising group that was planning a bush retreat with workshops on female sexuality, amongst other things. Thinking it might do Julia good to get out of town for a weekend she suggested they go together.

Julia prevaricated, unsure she wanted to spend an entire weekend with strangers. She distrusted women more than she distrusted men. With men at least she knew their motives. But once Susanna had the idea in her head she persisted and Julia eventually agreed to go.

The support she received at the retreat when she told her story, the friendships she made, the fun she had, the bonhomie of the evening singalongs, hilarious anecdotes, dancing and games and the calm of the bush went a long way to restoring her faith in women. It banished her childhood guilt. It saved her life.

Return

When she returned to the city she was determined to reclaim her space in the world. She would be her own master. She had started to like herself. She went about rebuilding her self-esteem methodically, articulating and attending to the matters that made life worthwhile, rejecting or simply avoiding those she considered destructive. Celibacy was now her practice. On a commonplace level she began to enjoy her days. But it wasn't until she met Frank that she began to trust men again.

His memory of their romantic involvement differed from her own. He claimed to have spent months of reconnaissance, preparing the groundwork for a successful encounter which, when it happened, was precipitous and more passionate than he could have imagined. But she recalled it differently. She didn't readily abandon her celibacy. Sex seemed to be a form of punishment. She wanted that to change but she wasn't going to be impulsive or reckless. She understood how delicate it needed to be if she were to achieve what others proclaimed of sex: joy, pleasure, love. She took her time.

They went to the movies together a few times and dined out afterwards at an Italian restaurant around the corner in Lygon Street, where they reviewed the movie earnestly and drank enough coffee to keep them awake all night discussing their favourite film genres. Frank had an interest in American anti-war movies, such as *Dr Strangelove, the Deer Hunter* and *Apocalypse Now,* while Julia loved anything French, especially French New Wave's François Truffaut and Jean-Luc Godard. She hated Hollywood remakes of her favourite films, refusing to see *Breathless,* starring Richard Gere, when Frank suggested it.

Their first fuck followed a movie one winter's night after watching the director's cut of the Japanese movie, *In the Realm of the Senses.*

'You won't be too anxious, I hope,' she said as she led him into her bedroom, alluding to the asphyxiation and genital mutilation in the penultimate scene. Her laughter was a release for both of them.

She could tell straight away that he was inexperienced, which pleased her. She took control, guided him in ways to pleasure her. She liked his lean physique and took her time exploring it.

Convolution

For the first time in her life she began to enjoy sex. Frank was obviously enjoying it as well and began to think it had some wider significance. Within six months he was suggesting it was time to meet their respective families.

She baulked. A reconciliation with her family was never going to happen, nor an introduction to his family. She gave no explanation for her obstinacy and he had the good sense not to badger her. In her own time she would speak about it.

When they started living together he encountered similar resistance to the suggestion they get a dog. He wanted to engender some sense of family with its illusion of permanency. A pet would have been a modest start. To make his proposal more appealing he said they could 'rescue a puppy' from the Lost Dogs' Home, but she began to cry and fearful of what lay behind her tears, he desisted.

She became involved with feminist politics and her social world expanded considerably. Her long-lost geniality gradually reappeared, but the emotional support she needed from day to day came almost entirely from Frank.

When Frank had recovered sufficiently from the assault they went away, first on a trip through Central Australia to Darwin, visiting the iconic tourist destinations along the way—Coober Pedy, Uluru, Kakadu —and later overseas to Europe.

The trip through Australia left her feeling ambivalent about her country, shocked by the deprivations of the indigenous population and moved by defiant attempts to retain its ancient culture. Frank shared her outrage at some of the living conditions they saw around Alice Springs and the tragedy of alcoholism in the Aboriginal communities, which seemed to both of them the quagmire into which anyone could stumble if they lost their identity and self-esteem. They felt ashamed that their civilization had desecrated the most ancient culture on Earth.

Europe, then, was a respite.

Julia felt she had more in common with the disgruntled Brits, the reserved Germans, the flamboyant Italians, the loquacious Greeks than with most of the Australians they had encountered in the outback. Sharing an interest in the visual arts dating back to their high school days when art classes were the fun periods for both of them, they visited many of the major art museums on the continent—the Uffizi, the Louvre, the Vatican, the Prado—and, in London, the Tate. In Rome they visited a house near the Spanish Steps where Keats spent his final months. In Paris they went to the Left Bank and the Café de Flore, to visit the haunts of Sartre and De Beauvoir. When they returned to England, Julia suggested they stay in London for a year or two. They got jobs in pubs and found a tiny flat above a laundrette in Hammersmith. But by Christmas and all through winter they froze. She couldn't bear the bitter cold. When Frank came down with pneumonia, Julia panicked. As soon as he recovered she bought tickets home. It was 1989.

So much time together and such reliance upon each other fostered a sense of mutual destiny. They were meant for each other. Julia believed it. Frank was happy to accept it when she spoke about their closeness, which he liked to think of as *family*. They rented flats in Melbourne's northern suburbs until they had enough money for a deposit on a house in North Coburg. She filled it with objects she loved. She designed the garden. Frank contributed a few sentimental bits and pieces but was willing to cede responsibility for its appearance, its ambience, to Julia, as long as it kept her happy. A happy Julia meant satisfying sex, which mattered to Frank even when it became routine. The way their bodies merged! The intimacy was oneness. The oneness, love. If other people considered them inseparable he took it as a compliment.

Twenty five years transpired in the blink of an eye.

A perplexing condition

Outside the dog barked again, more urgently, and Julia imagined Cliff prowling the streets nearby, restless, a grim digression in a testosteronal odyssey. He wasn't the sort to jerk off. He would have found it humiliating. She cupped her vulva again and squeezed her thighs around the hand, closed her eyes and groaned, the sound of indecision.

At breakfast she sat alone and nibbled the edges of her toast until Cliff approached, bleary-eyed and rather jaundiced. He suggested a morning run along the beach.

In alarmingly identical tracksuits they jogged in silence for a couple of kilometres. They could easily have been mistaken for a well-established couple. Smaller waves than yesterday eased onto the beach. The sky was subdued.

As they approached the mouth of a creek, Cliff spoke.

'Come on, then.' He looked at his watch. He would be leading the morning workshop in less than an hour. 'A race to the creek before we turn back, okay?'

She got the jump on him, sprinted ahead, with Cliff protesting about her unfairness. Laughter hindered her enough to allow him to catch her. He grabbed her waist and they tumbled onto the sand, breathless and aching from the fun of it. When he manoeuvred her beneath him and tried to kiss her she managed to cover his mouth with her hand.

'I've been thinking about this—us—all night,' she said, barely able to breathe with his weight on her. 'Before any of this, Cliff, I have to meet your wife.'

He raised himself on his arms to observe her in puzzlement. 'What? Why?'

'I want to know what the woman you're being unfaithful to is like before I can do this.'

She felt the force of an incredulous guffaw on her face. He sat up on the sand and looked askance at her. 'You're joking?'

'No.'

He cast his gaze to the sea as she stood and began to brush sand from her tracksuit. 'Then I want to meet your bloke too, what's his name, Frank, is it?' he voiced after some thought unable to completely conceal his anger.

What she cherished

Cliff's response disappointed Julia. He might consider spouses irrelevant in the planning and execution of an infidelity but Frank had been her partner for more than a quarter of a century. Even if her love for him was changing and now seemed more a tepid fraternal fondness than the feeling shared by lovers, there was no denying how close they were, how intertwined their lives had become, how dependent they had been over the years, not just emotionally but in most aspects of their livelihood, sharing budgets, chattels and debts, becoming—if you could overlook their childlessness—a family. She had probably never announced it to her friends, not even to Frank, but it was certainly how she felt: a micro-family.

She already thought that way by the time they returned from overseas. Nothing broke or consolidated relationships like travel in exotic lands. They had got along so well, complemented each other so that one's weaknesses were the other's strengths. Frank's orienteering skills. Julia's ease with strangers. Frank's good sense with money. Julia's nose for the weird and wonderful that made their trips unforgettable.

When they returned to Melbourne, while Julia did odd jobs here and there, it was Frank who took work more seriously, starting his controversial career with an independent but high-profile inner-suburban weekly paper after he submitted a quirky piece on the youthful fringe culture around Fitzroy and Collingwood, one of the few cadets to slip into the industry in the nineties without a degree in journalism.

The dinner party

When she arranged a dinner party a week after the weekend retreat, Julia also invited Professor Petrus and a couple of her other colleagues to create the impression it was work related, one of those things an academic had to do to consolidate tenure.

'You were just away with them recently,' Frank protested, no fan of dinner parties. 'On some junket. For tax purposes, wasn't it? Can you get deductions for dinner parties too? I should start having a few.'

'You're forgetting, dude, you don't pay taxes anymore.'

Shocked at her bluntness he blinked, unable to respond.

'This is important, Frank. There's a lectureship coming up soon.'

'Oh, yes, of course. I forgot about your ambitions.'

'Fuck, Frank! I don't ask much of you. One of us has to have a job, you know.'

'Don't worry, I'll be there, the perfect silent partner.'

'It's up to you whether you're silent or not. These people aren't elitist, you know.'

'I'll put that to the test, shall I?'

'Oh, Frank, grow up! Don't be so petty.'

She didn't ask for his help with the preparations. He didn't offer.

The professor arrived first alone. He was a widower. His wife had died of breast cancer a few years earlier and as far as Julia knew he had taken no steps towards remarrying. She led him into the living room and introduced him to Frank before excusing herself to continue with her culinary preparations.

The professor looked ill at ease. 'Julia tells me you want to be a writer.'

'I am already,' Frank corrected defensively. 'I've been a journalist all my life.'

'Ah, yes, she told me you've been retrenched or something. Difficult time for journalists. New era, eh?'

'I still have a commission in the pipeline and a bit of freelance.'

'Had anything published besides journalistic stuff?'

'Not much.'

'What then?'

'Long time ago. A short story. Published in a national newspaper I worked for at the time.'

'Which, may I ask?'

'The *National Times.*'

'Ah, yes. I remember the *National Times.* Went out of circulation years ago. Australians are too anti-intellectual for that kind of journal. What was it about?'

'The story?' Frank hesitated. He was no longer proud of it. 'About the way smokers were being ostracised. It was supposed to be a satire. Like thought police, there were anti-smoking police. It was based on Kafka's *The Trial*, sort of. *Someone had it in for F, for without having done anything wrong–*. My protagonist woke up to find his cigarettes confiscated, the anti-smoking police in the next room waiting to interrogate him—something like that.'

'Are you a smoker?'

'Me? No, no. Well, I was in those days. Weren't we all? I was defending the right to smoke. These days I have a different opinion on the topic.'

The professor sniggered silently, at him or the changing times Frank couldn't tell. Either way he felt miffed.

'Anything else?'

'Well, at the end of it, my smoker dies *at sunset like a snake* rather than *like a dog* as in *The Trial*–you are familiar with *The Trial*, aren't you?–and *as if the vice* rather than *the shame would outlast him*. I thought it clever at the time and I guess the paper did too. But now I'm not so sure. The best part about it, I thought, was the accompanying illustration by a cartoonist whose name I've forgotten, unfortunately–I have a problem with names–Gestapo anti-smoking forces goose-stepping past an unhealthy-looking smoker hiding under a bridge in pyjamas.'

'No, no,' Petrus interrupted, his eyelids closing wantonly, always impatient with anyone who misinterpreted him. 'Anything else? Any other publications?' And his last utterance was enunciated slowly as if he were introducing a new word to a child. 'Any real books?'

'I've written a couple in my spare time. But I haven't found a publisher yet, although I've had some rather flattering rejection letters, you know, *the prose is vivid, we'd love to publish this, it deserves a broad readership, but our finance department*–or whatever the bean counters in the publishing house are called–always have the final say, *try another*–that sort of thing.' Frank was desperate to talk of anything else. 'Anyway, how's your research going?'

He knew that when Julia told people about his desire to be an author she was only trying to impress them. Her partner was not the dull, taciturn, uninteresting hack-reporter that he often appeared to be. There was potential beneath the bland exterior. But it embarrassed him. It humiliated him when they asked politely about his writing and he had nothing positive to say.

It got worse. She was quite willing to disclose the struggles he was having, the technical difficulties he faced about which he had spoken to her in private. Her intention was never to shame him. She simply wanted people to understand his commitment to the craft.

The professor, relieved to have the opportunity to talk about his latest research, his lips protruding earnestly and eyes turned towards the ceiling, was well into his preamble when the doorbell rang. Frank turned and left him mid-delivery, not that the professor seemed to notice immediately for he was off on a tangent about what made the research so fascinating.

As Frank reached the front door he heard Julia approaching behind, rapid steps that drew a quizzical look from him. 'I can get it,' she said, her voice betraying her anxiety.

His eyebrows rose wondering about her enthusiasm, noticing she wore the crimson dress in which she appeared now and then in his dreams.

She halted, a little flushed.

Cliff Rogerson stood on the porch with his wife. A charming smile animated his goatee. 'You mus' be Frank.' A hand was extended towards him. 'Cliff Rog'son. And my wife, Sraah.'

'Sraah?'

'Oh, for Christ's sake, Cliffy!' The short woman standing beside him blew smoke from a rollie towards the night. 'Sarah,' she enunciated clearly.

'Hi, Cliff,' Julia said affectedly over Frank's shoulder. 'Hi, Sarah, I'm Julia.'

There was a lop-sided smile on Sarah's chubby face. 'Two flutes of champas is all it takes,' she said with a tilt of her head towards her husband. 'Pleased to meet you.' She offered her hand to Julia, around Frank, who stepped sideways to facilitate the greeting. The cigarette was jammed between her lips. Her other hand was tugging a sleeve of her husband's suit. 'Needs the social lubrication.'

Julia stared. There was something odd about her. It was the scar that extended from her forehead to her chin, disfiguring her eyelids on one side, and the way the same side of her torso drooped as if the scar continued the length of her body, an unsuccessful dissection. As a distraction her hair was dyed bright orange.

'Come in, please,' Julia urged when her husband's good manners failed. And to Frank: 'You shouldn't leave George by himself too long.'

'I don't suppose you allow smokers inside?' said Sarah, her voice fatalistic.

'Smokers, yes,' Julia said over her shoulder as she retreated towards the kitchen. 'Smoking, no.'

'I'll get you an ashtray,' Frank offered.

'Don't worry.' Sarah flicked her butt into the garden. 'I'll give you a hand,' she called to Julia.

In the kitchen Julia checked the oven.

'Nice kitchen,' Sarah said, placing a couple of bottles of wine on the speckled stone bench. 'You like cooking?'

'Sometimes. It's a diversion. I needed it as a counterbalance. Give the brain a rest.'

'I hate it. We eat out a lot. Mind if I taste this?' She didn't wait for an answer, taking one of the hors d'oeuvres from its plate, licking her thumb after she had finished. 'Smoked oysters. How original! Has he rooted you yet?'

Julia shut the oven door, blushing. 'I beg your pardon?'

'Cliffy. Has he got into your pants?'

Julia didn't dare look at Sarah, fearing her face would betray her. 'I hardly know him. He's fairly new to our Department. We're just work colleagues. We have a professional relationship.'

'I know what *professional* requires these days.' Sarah chuckled. 'I bet he's tried. You're pretty. Beautiful hair. Svelte. He likes your type. Weren't you away on that retreat a couple of weeks ago?'

'As a matter of fact I was, but—'

'There you go then. Don't tell me he didn't try. We've been married ten years. I know what he's like and what he likes.'

'How can you afford eating out all the time?'

Sarah chuckled, a husky sound thanks to the damage cigarettes had done to her throat. 'You don't have to worry about me,' she said. 'I'm used to his infidelities. Who he fucks is of no interest to me. Unless it becomes serious. Then I'm prepared to ruin reputations.'

Julia was suddenly angry, surprising herself, hoping it wasn't on display. Nevertheless she glared at Sarah who returned her gaze without abandoning the smug, drooping smile. 'I'm sorry you feel that way,' Julia said coolly, not the least intimidated now. 'But you're being incredibly presumptuous!'

'Am I?'

'Whatever happened to your face if you don't mind me asking? You look like you've been carved up.'

Sarah's smile endured as she appraised her host. 'Sooner or later we all get carved up by someone, darling. But your husband seems a nice bloke.' She picked up the tray of hors d'oeuvres. 'Shall I take him one of these?'

While they were in the kitchen others had arrived. Dr Sophie Kokinos, her partner, Andreas Marin, and a young doctoral student, Peter Harding, who had also been invited along by

Julia to repay him for some invaluable advice he had given her at a crucial stage of her own research. He looked shy and out of place. After accepting a glass of wine, he found somewhere to stand alone, away from the probability of small talk, near the wood heater with its warmth.

Julia smiled at him when she entered the room but crossed to Kokinos, who kissed her cheeks and handed her a box of Swiss chocolates.

'You look gorgeous tonight,' Kokinos whispered. 'Anyone would think you're hoping to make out, darling.' She puckered her lips, which were an incendiary crimson, and rolled her eyes as their languid lids came down. Like a drum skin her throat vibrated, emitting a guttural sound.

A deep blush garnished Julia's cheeks and ears. 'You, too, dear. But keep your eyes off the professor. He's mine.'

A guffaw and snort. Kokinos clutched Julia to steady herself. 'Oh, Jesus, I'm wildly jealous.'

'Shh! Shh! This is a serious dinner party.'

'Glad to hear it, gal. Where can I get a drink?'

'Frank'll get you one.'

Julia called to Frank who was standing near the French window with Rogerson and Petrus. She noticed Sarah had crossed to Peter, who was looking uncomfortable, corralled between her and the wood heater, accepting a smoked oyster in the hope she would move away.

Petrus was speaking to Rogerson who was feigning an interest, nodding judiciously while looking at her.

When Sarah moved away from Peter, Julia went over to him. 'How's it going?'

'I haven't had a chance to speak to the professor yet,' he said wistfully.

'It may not happen, unless you've got something praiseworthy to say. The old boy has a habit of rabbiting on about his latest research on these occasions.'

'I thought that's what this was about.'

His forlorn demeanour moved Julia who was reminded of a young Frank trying to impress people whose approval he craved. 'Not exactly,' she said, squeezing his arm. 'More of an unwinding thing now the research is finished. But that won't stop him.'

She was right. Petrus was in an expansive mood. Once all were seated at the dinner table and Julia had served the main course, a baked eggplant dish whose recipe she had found on the internet, the professor talked for a long time about his research, which had investigated attitudes towards the burqa amongst non-Muslims according to the socio-economic status of respondents. What pleased the professor most of all was that the government had expressed an interest in his preliminary findings. There was without a doubt evidence that intolerance and regional demographic factors had a strong correlation. The western suburbs of Melbourne and Sydney showed far more hostility towards the burqa than the residents of the leafy suburbs of either city, although he admitted some of the evidence was 'patchy'.

'No mention of class in your analysis, professor?' said Frank, surprising the academics.

'Class consciousness is not really a part of anyone's mindset these days, or very few, but I take your point.'

'Too true.' Frank stabbed his roasted eggplant with a fork. 'Those few you mention, Prof, they're all ageing die-hard lefties, wouldn't you say? Bolshily, yeah, that's a word, don't laugh, bolshily refusing to abandon ideals that date back to their student days, who are finding it tremendously difficult, almost impossible to move into our glorious, exciting, yet bewildering, uncertain twenty-first century.' His eyes moved steadily from one face to the next, an urbane smile tempering his antagonism, pleased with the attention he was receiving until his gaze reached the professor. 'Not many of them were ever really part of the working class but they longed to be and still do. They're about the only ones who do. Still you have to feel you belong somewhere, don't you, Prof? What about yourself? Any preferences? My problem is I've got no idea where I belong any more or even where I want to belong since my preferred option has apparently disappeared. At my age you'd think I'd have worked that out by now. But that has nothing to do with whether class exists or not, does it, Prof?'

'They make good use of social media,' Sarah interjected, elbow on the table, one hand propping up her jaw, fork playing with her food. 'That's twenty-first century.'

'Who're you talkin' 'bout?' said her husband, baffled, querulous, and looking for more wine.

'The old lefties. But that was never your scene, was it, Cliffy, darls? Was it yours, Frank?'

'I've always been a journalist—the fourth estate.'

'Oh, I see, outside—above—the class system.'

The professor intervened. 'My methodology deliberately avoids a class analysis.'

'What does class mean anyway?' This was Peter trying hard to contribute to the conversation. 'If you take the classic Marxist definition, the relationship of an individual to the means of production, then most working people have a foot on either side of the class divide these days.'

'Painful,' said Sarah. 'It's as sharp as razor wire. Potentially emasculating.'

'How do you figure that?' said Kokinos, addressing Peter.

'How many Australians hold equity in companies, either directly through a portfolio or indirectly through their superannuation funds?' He spoke self-consciously, knowing all now had their eyes on him. 'With super funds investing in all sorts of companies, that makes the average Australian part owner of the means of production as well as a wage earner.'

'No wonder they occasionally feel schizoid,' said Sarah.

Petrus tapped the handle of his knife on the table with the gravitas of a presiding judge. 'Let's not stray too far from the main issue here. Class has become such an obsolete concept it's no longer a useful academic tool, as young Peter implies. Social relations have become far too complex altogether. We need to be looking for new paradigms.'

It wasn't what Peter was implying but he didn't contradict him.

'The ruling class would just love that argument,' said Frank after a mouthful of wine, slopping some onto his shirt which was overstretched across his paunch, its buttons struggling to prevent a disaster, 'while laughing all the way to the bank.'

'I gathered that was what you were implying,' the professor said.

Frank noticed Petrus was talking to him but eyeing Julia. More wine.

'What we have been researching is xenophobia,' the professor declared, 'which has a tendency to manifest in the most economically vulnerable individuals, those who feel threatened by new arrivals, especially immigrants who look different, who have the most visual impact, women of the burqa, for example, who become easy targets of vilification. It's a misplaced fear, of course. These women are no threat to white unemployed males. To the contrary. But they become the scapegoats for all the resentments and anxieties this underclass experiences.'

'Under*class*! Ahah!' Frank almost sprang from his chair. 'We can't escape a class analysis, can we?' He pointed his knife at the professor. 'It's a pity our dear departed comrade, Doctor Charles Johnson, isn't here. Did you know him, Prof? No?

He'd tell you a thing or two about class. He'd recite *Das Kapital* backwards for you if you asked nicely, not to mention the entire oeuvre of Comrade Trotsky to which he had–if you don't mind me saying so, Julia, since he was your friend foremost–to which he had an indecent sentimental attachment. You should have seen his bookshelves! Ye gods! None of the libraries in the Kremlin, or the CIA I'd hazard a guess, had more tomes devoted to communism. Theory, history, dialectics, dossiers, you name it. By the way, I don't know about CIA headquarters, which at one time would have had more experts on Marxist-Leninism than existed in the entire Eastern Bloc, but in the Kremlin there was not a word spoken or written by Trotsky. His books were used to fuel old Comrade Joe's samovar.'

Julia glared at him. 'Stop being facetious, Frank. You know how dear and important Charlie was to me. He may not be with us anymore but that's no reason to mock him.'

'Mock Charlie? To the contrary, there's no-one living today I respect more than Charlie, even if he is dead. I wish he were here. He'd bring some intellectual manna to the table. By the way, did you know this?' Frank rubbed his belly which seemed to be expanding by the minute as he waited for the curiosity to build. 'My wife–sorry, my partner–accompanied Charlie on a pilgrimage to Trotsky's grave, didn't you, darling, without me, all the way to Mexico. Didn't want me along. Didn't think I'd be respectful enough or something.'

Julia got to her feet. 'Can you give me a hand to clear these plates, Frank?'

'Certainly, dear.'

In the kitchen the hostile clatter of plates told Frank he was in some sort of trouble. Sheepishly he waited for Julia to speak.

'I won't have you insulting my boss, who happens also to be a friend. You're making a fool of yourself. Why, I have no idea. Stop drinking so much. You're being obnoxious.'

'Oh, so now you're issuing orders.'

'Don't be so fucking puerile, Frank. These people are my peers.'

'Except the weird looking woman. She's just married to one of 'em. Same status as me, I guess. And that other bloke, husband of the other professor.'

'Partner, not husband, like us Frank.' She stared, genuinely disappointed in him. 'Is that what's eating you up? You're feeling intellectually threatened.'

'By that pompous twerp? Hardly. And that other bloke, he's hardly opened his mouth. Who is he? I can't even remember his name.'

'You don't remember anybody's name, Frank. Which one? Sophie's husband, Andreas, or Cliff Rogerson? He's only been with the department a short while. But he's incredibly intelligent.'

'I hadn't noticed. More of a masculine threat than an intellectual one, I would say.'

The fire went out of Julia.

'What is he, a sommelier or something?' Frank continued. 'Spends most of his time sampling our wines.'

'God, you can talk. Besides they brought two bottles.'

'Let's hope he sticks to that then.'

Her energy dissipated like cooking vapours. Perhaps her feelings weren't as hidden as she supposed. She wondered if he had perceived something, a surreptitious look that had passed between her and Cliff, an unintended nuance in her voice when she spoke directly to him.

'Try to sober up a bit,' she said, subdued. 'I know you'll regret this in the morning. Please, Frank, don't ruin the evening for me.'

She left the kitchen but was back immediately. 'By the way, the professor's name is George. For God's sake stop calling him Prof. Have you any idea how demeaning that is?'

She returned to the dining room where the discussion had segued to the threat of Islamism. Her emotions were in turmoil. She longed for Cliff's hands between her legs. And there was Sarah, saying little, but boldly swapping her gaze from husband to Julia with an unnerving sardonic smile. This woman thrives on mayhem, Julia guessed.

'A lot of these young Muslim men who turn to terrorism are petty criminals, or have been. Drugs. Armed robbery. Assault. Suddenly they are given what they see as a dignified outlet for their violence against a country that has only ever allowed them to be delinquents. They see Australia and the West as playgrounds of the Devil. Attack their citizens, you attack the Devil, no matter how harmless those you kill or maim may be.'

Petrus paused to place his cutlery on his empty plate, the last to finish eating.

'If you want to rid Australia of terrorism,' he continued after wiping his chin with a serviette, 'there's only one way to do it and it's not better intelligence, not more surveillance, not more security at airports and sporting stadiums, although all these play a role. It's to give these young men opportunities to build a dignified life. Education. Jobs. Give them a way to escape their hopeless lives. It'll require a lot of government funding but not as much as the cost of terrorism in the long run. That'll be my recommendation to government.'

'Won't be very popular with the voters,' said Rogerson, joining the conversation for the first time, holding up a bottle to see if it contained more wine.

Petrus waved his hand dismissively. 'I know, I know, but that's not my business. A good politician should be able to persuade his constituency what is good for it.'

'Her,' said Sarah.

'I beg your pardon?' Petrus frowned.

'*Her* constituency. A *good* politician is more likely to be female.' Her laughter was vapid. The other women smiled. 'The terrorists who flew into the World Trade Center and the Pentagon weren't exactly delinquents from decaying suburbs,' she added.

The professor was losing his patience. 'I'm talking about the terrorists or would-be terrorists we see in Australia. Generally speaking they are young from low socio-economic backgrounds with little or no self-esteem and easily manipulated by fanatics and ideologues.'

'Well, what about the Americans?' interjected Frank who had just returned to the table and in a clumsy manoeuvre reached between Julia and the professor for a bottle of wine, a towel wrapped around his head.

Everyone stopped talking and drinking to stare at him, incredulously or in umbrage it was hard to tell. Only Sarah laughed.

Frank rounded the table to Rogerson to pour him another wine. 'Are you a sommelier by any chance?'

'What are you doing, Frank?' cried Julia. 'What are you trying to prove?'

'What's America's responsibility for all this?' he persisted, ignoring her, moving to his seat. 'Who created all this chaos in the Middle East? What about the Palestinian question? Don't tell me the humiliation of the Palestinians isn't behind all the extremism we're seeing today. More than half a century of occupation. The Americans are allowing Israel to get away with genocide here.'

'Ah, so the towels supposed to show your allegiance to the Palestinians,' Sarah interjected between snorts of humour, 'and not oppressed Moslem women?'

'Precisely,' he said uncertainly, removing the towel, suddenly feeling foolish and suspecting he had drunk too much, too quickly.

'I must say you do a good impression of Yasser Arafat,' she added.

'He died long ago, alas,' said Frank. 'I had the good fortune to interview him once.'

Julia had her eyes closed and was trying to control her breathing.

'My research shows hostility towards the burqa is seen as an insult to Islam,' the professor continued, adding another layer of gravitas to his voice, ignoring Frank, 'despite the Koran stating nothing specific about attire except that women should dress modestly. Nevertheless, these young Muslim men see any criticism of the burqa as an attack on their religion. It allows them to feel righteous about the violence they wish to perpetrate against a world that has left them behind.'

While attention was on the professor's words, Julia glanced at Rogerson, hoping Frank's absurd behaviour hadn't diminished his desire for her. His eyes signalled his lack of interest in the entire scene, drolly indicating he wanted to disappear with her, using repetitive sideways glances at the door.

She grinned despite her fury at Frank dominating her other emotions. With a barely visible shake of her head she declined his offer, closing her eyes and privately relishing his suggestion. She pressed a fist into her groin beneath the tablecloth.

Frank was getting drunker. He gesticulated perilously close to Sarah's head and demanded an audience. 'How I wish Comrade Charlie was here! He'd be able to explain things more clearly than I. What a mind he had! What a vast reserve of knowledge! Anything you wanted to know about British and French colonialism in the Middle East, Zionism, Yasser Arafat, the PLO, Hamas, the Ba'ath Party of Iraq, Saddam Hussein, the Ayatollah Khomeini, Al Qaeda, Osama bin Laden, Wahhabism, even the Prophet himself, the Saudis, George Bush Senior and George Double-ya, you name it, he had an encyclopaedic knowledge of the facts. All right, he was a communist. So what? Nobody was more disappointed in the form it took in the twentieth century than Charlie. But he has never been ashamed to call himself a communist or a Marxist. He was proud of it, actually. Me? I've never been a communist. A socialist maybe. An anarchist when I was younger. These days, who knows? I'm just anti-this, anti-that. Revolution? You're joking. Get ready for a thousand years of capitalism. That's why I feel so pessimistic these days.'

No-one else had mentioned revolution. In fact no-one else had said anything for some moments. The others at the table were now watching him uneasily, wondering if it was time to leave, before the man became hysterical or violent. He noticed and nodded slowly as if realising he had achieved his goal which was their undivided attention.

'Charlie was the wisest and most honest bloke I've ever known. Such a crying shame he died so young.' His voice was getting maudlin.

'Frank.' Julia, who realised her fury had to wait, reached across the table to squeeze his forearm as he held onto an empty wine bottle. 'I loved Charlie too, but this's not the time—'

'Why not?'

'You know as well as I do he'd hate us talking about him like this at a dinner party.'

'So why have a dinner party today of all days?' Frank took another gulp of wine, upset. 'I want to talk about him. I miss him. I miss him more than I ever thought I would. Especially tonight. God knows we had our differences politically but he never let that interfere with our friendship. How many people you know are like that? I had a lot of respect for him. He never worried about what others thought of him. He just stuck to his guns—his principles I mean.'

'Frank.'

'No, no. Let me finish.'

'No-one else here knew him.'

'Well, what's wrong with talking about him? He was your friend too. He's only been dead a year.'

'I know.'

'A year today, exactly, in fact, ladies and gentlemen.'

'Frank, please.'

'He died the day before my birthday, did you know? Did any of you know? The inconsiderate bastard. Typical communist. No thought for the individual!'

'Frank.'

'Dead. He's crossed that terrifying line. We've all got to face it one day. Being a good Marxist he didn't believe in the afterlife.' He looked around at the guests. 'Do any of you? Does it scare you? It scares the hell out of me. None of that religious stuff makes any sense to me. I've given this a lot of thought lately. If there is a god, why did the fucker go to the trouble of creating life out of chemicals of all things, because that's what we are folks—every cell, every hair, every nerve, our eyes, arms, brain, every last bit of us, all just chemical combinations and nothing else—it's the only thing we can be certain of about ourselves—the only verifiable thing—and then this god fellow somehow inserts a soul, this spiritual thing, this very un-chemical, unverifiable thing, into the chemical mixture that is me and you, only to deconstruct us after a few short years and send our souls to eternity. Why go to all that trouble? You academics would've heard of Occam's razor, surely? No, no, don't get up. It's not time to go yet. I'm leaning towards Comrade Charlie's view that the soul is a delusion coming straight out of a terror of our impending non-existence. After being aware you're alive who wants to die? Well, maybe a few sad fuckers. But in the end we're all just going to decompose into some other less egotistical type of chemical soup. Any of you here theologians? Maybe you can explain it to me.'

He stood to look around again for another bottle of wine.

The guests were all staring at the table. The only one watching him was Petrus. 'Now—the *burqa*!' the professor insisted and everyone except Frank and Julia burst into laughter.

'I haven't finished yet.' Frank slopped more wine into his glass and offered the bottle to others. Rogerson accepted it.

Julia spoke. 'Frank, please—'

'There's a lot you can criticise about Marxism and I'm absolutely certain, as academics, right, you all take a position on it, pro or con—but one thing at least in its favour—are any of yous listening?' He gulped some wine. 'One thing—it gives you somewhere to belong. You're a Marxist, it's a global fraternity, comrades. Doesn't matter if you know each other, you've got this unbreakable bond, well, within limits, there are different strands, isn't there? Stalinist, Trotskyist, Maoist, etcetera. But this society we live in—there's nowhere to belong, so people attach themselves to a football club or a church or something or there's this phoney nationalism— Ozzie, Ozzie, Ozzie—it's all crap. It's a peripheral and phoney type of belonging. We have a great yearning to belong some- where but all of us are alone. You lot, maybe you think you belong to *The Academy* or some such esoteric group of intellectuals, and maybe I thought I belonged to something similar, *the fourth estate*. But not anymore and not just because I've been made redundant. It's this fucking world! I belong nowhere. Good night.'

Frank strode from the room.

An awkward silence followed as if someone had just brazened a loud fart or confessed to wanting their tiresome old mother dead. The diners picked up napkins to pat their mouths or sniffed their wine with sudden curiosity.

As host and partner of the pariah Julia felt obliged to intervene. 'Sorry everyone.' She tried to sound cheerful. 'But you can understand why Frank's a bit maudlin. A terrible thing, having a dear friend die. This is the first anniversary. He doesn't usually drink so much.'

Kokinos threw up her hands in an ironic gesture of bafflement. 'Personally I don't understand why *any* woman or man for that matter would want to wear a burqa, can you?'

This animated the group and the discussion moved on to the arguments pro and con the burqa which continued for the next half hour and on through brandied cumquats and ice cream, which Julia intended Frank to serve but in his absence did so herself.

Later as coffee arrived conversations broke up into personal gripes about university policies and weekend plans.

'I should be going,' said Petrus. 'I've got an early flight tomorrow. TV appearance in Perth of all places.'

The other guests took this as a signal and rose in unison.

As they made their way towards the front door Rogerson stepped up to Julia. 'By the way,' he said, his vinous breath causing her to drawn back from him a little. 'Here's that book I promised you.'

She looked puzzled as he handed it to her but regained her composure quickly and accepted it. 'Oh, yes, thanks.'

He gave her a peck on the cheek as he left and so did his wife, who smiled meaningfully and said, 'Enjoy.'

Julia blinked. Sarah tapped the book.

'Oh, yes, of course,' Julia mumbled.

The fateful note

Once everyone was gone and Frank was in the toilet, vomiting, she looked inside the cover and found a note. *Meet me tomorrow, 10am. I want to take you somewhere in the Dandenongs. Please! I'm in love. Text me rendezvous.* There was a phone number. She wondered why he hadn't simply texted her himself, and then remembered she'd deliberately with-held her number at the retreat for fear of where it might lead.

She sat for a long time in the living room pondering the ambiguity in *take you*, troubled by the sexism in both its meanings and dazed by the declaration of love. She nursed the book, *Infinite Jest*. For a moment she suspected the title was part of the message.

She texted him. *Ok. The Lounge Lizard. xxx.*

Panic surged through her chest towards her throat, which constricted to prevent any audible expression. A scream? Surely not. It would have been more of a whine. Her SMS response had been reckless. *Ok* was not a problem but under the circumstances *xxx* was a signal she hadn't intended to give. She had ceded too much ground. And the *take you* lingered like an omen.

Frank's noisy presence in the bathroom reminded her what was at stake.

She reclined her neck into the yielding headrest and took comfort from the soft corrugations of the fabric until the room began to spin. Unlike Frank she hadn't drunk too much but perhaps more than usual. She had to open her eyes to fasten the world before it flung her beyond its orbit.

Leaning forward to focus on the floor, whose rug, with a design of dancing amoebic shapes reminiscent of Miró, seemed to express the state of her consciousness until the image of Rogerson's wife emerged. Sarah. What a strange creature! Neither beautiful nor charming. Amoebic in some ways. Nothing redeeming unless one considered the ability to intimidate a virtue. Orange hair to divert attention from her disfigurement. She seemed to have survived an attempt to cleave her in two. Was Rogerson the culprit? A wannabe axe murderer? She implied it, didn't she? Or was that just Julia's trepidation. Oh, God, drink too much and the mind reverts to melodrama! More likely something mundane like a car accident. They seemed an ill-suited couple, he an intellectual, she an anti-intellectual with a caustic wit willing to tear apart the man she had no intention of leaving. Julia found herself feeling protective of Rogerson, forming an emotional allegiance, willing to give him what he wanted just to antagonise his virulent wife.

She buried her face in her hands and groaned, unable to decide what *she* wanted, knowing she shouldn't even try in her current intoxicated state but unable to stop herself thinking of her potential lover who at least, even drunk, had maintained some decorum. She remembered holding his cock a week earlier, jerking him off. The convulsion still lingered across the palm of her hand. She tried to imagine what her life would be like if she started an affair with him. Could she count on him being discreet? Did she even want an affair? The secrecy it required was anathema to her. It went against all her principles. And it mattered to her that people would think her a hypocrite. Why should she hide what she felt? Could she tell Frank she just needed someone to fuck but didn't want to leave him? Was that how Cliff and Sarah had arranged their marriage? She knew Frank would accept it. But to live with him afterwards while he endured his humiliation stoically? It was something she knew she couldn't stay around to watch. Could she break with Frank after all these years? She still loved him. But when the ardour vanished from their sexual encounters, which she assumed was inevitable after so many years together, it transformed the love she felt to something akin to companionable affection while sex became just another domestic chore. It shocked her to admit it. She couldn't recall the last time

Frank had managed to bring her to orgasm although now and then she pretended in order to assuage the sense of inadequacy that prolonged his wearisome humping. Was it right to continue living with someone when the sex was a charade? She knew he would suffer if she abandoned him. A late middle-aged man left alone. Frank was not the type to find another partner easily. He would suffer and bear his suffering privately. She could see him standing before a microwave oven in a modest unit waiting for his frozen dinner to thaw, blaming himself for his solitary existence. It would be a cruelty that she had inflicted. Even the thought of it distressed her.

But what about herself, her own rights? With a jolt she realised she was again subjugating her own desires, her own needs, to another. How many years had she been railing against that kind of mentality? *Go ahead, fuck Cliff, if that's what you desire, and face the consequences honestly.* Surely everyone could live with that? Honesty was the key. Frank had said as much at the dinner party when he eulogized their friend, Charlie, whom they both considered a person of integrity. She wondered what Charlie would advise.

Interlude

Charlie, dead one year almost to the day. She was surprised she had forgotten he had died so near to Frank's birthday. She should have anticipated the emotional complexities and delayed the dinner party. In her haste to indulge an infatuation she had flouted her famous common sense, which Charlie had admired so much. It was one of the reasons he had befriended her and called her *comrade*.

They had met at a public rally against the proposed closure of the Upfield railway line. The closure was first mooted in the 1980s to develop a freeway along the rail corridor and floated again in the 1990s as part of a Western Bypass, motor vehicles instead of trains. There were other proposals for the line as well, such as a light rail along parts of it, but many locals who lived near the line wanted it maintained with significant upgrades to stations and crossings.

Charlie, who had once been a tram conductor and was a strong advocate of all forms of public transport, spoke at the rally. He had gained notoriety for his militancy during the historic conductors' strike, where trams were parked head-to-tail for kilometres along the streets of the central business district, which began in early 1990 after the State government decided conductors were no longer necessary. There were clashes between police and unionists. Charlie was one of the strikers arrested. The government eventually backed down but when a more conservative government was elected a couple of years later, all the conductors' jobs eventually disappeared. Refusing to accept a position within the Tramways as a ticket inspector, catching fare evaders who were making the most of the conductor-less trams, an unemployed Charlie became a popular government antagonist at public transport rallies.

Julia was just a spectator in the crowd but was impressed enough with his speech to approach him afterwards and offer her support. He gave her information on the next planning meeting of the Save the Upfield Line Committee and talked to her for a while about her reasons for wanting to be involved.

'I know how important it is to people who can't afford a car or who don't drive. Pensioners. The unemployed,' she said. 'Even if you've got a car it's the easiest way into the city. I use the train all the time.'

'Then you pass through my station,' he responded. 'Macaulay.'

The friendship grew out of a mutual respect for each other's no-nonsense approach to political activism, both believing in the importance of grass-roots involvement in the determination of policies for the local community. The Upfield campaign had been the start of their long association in community politics which, after its success, extended to public housing, bike paths, the defence of public land, community gardens, protecting the ecosystems along the local creeks and periodic support for socialist or green candidates in local, state and federal elections.

Julia wasn't far into her relationship with Frank, which still had periods of delight, and Charlie eventually met Meryl at a public housing support group who shared a few happy years with him before she suffered a fatal heart attack. Her death brought Julia and Charlie closer together. He needed emotional support although he would never have admitted it, considering personal tragedies inconsequential in the grand scheme of things, the mighty sweep of history. Frank and Charlie, after their initial antagonism, became closer too. Their political differences weren't gaping enough to prevent hours of animated discussion where respect for each other burgeoned, aided by Charlie's mellow humour and Frank's often belated but quirky repartee.

Charlie no longer belonged to a Marxist party. Most of the leftist parties around the edges of mainstream politics were splitting or disintegrating, consumed by the sophistry of their leaders who had little or no contact with the masses they claimed to represent. Charlie was convinced he could achieve more outside a party, at least until the social conditions were more conducive to revolution. Frank told him he'd be waiting a long time.

As his health deteriorated Charlie became more subdued, partly because tumours pressing against his ears were slowly rendering him deaf. When his comrades realised how serious his condition had become they rallied around him, offering him support at home, organising a working bee to clean inside and repair some of the external structures that had deteriorated over the years. He had completed his PhD on the political activities of the Communist Party of Australia in the union movement during the Menzies era but it had taken its toll on his health, and now his thesis was being published and he wanted to undertake a speaking tour to promote it, which seemed crazy to Julia but some of his friends encouraged him, declaring it an heroic contribution to the cause even if the cause had fizzled out decades before like sodden fireworks in the fanfare at the fall of the Berlin Wall. There's an imprecise line between heroism and folly. Debate about it could fill a book. His tour went ahead. It definitely hastened his death. It took a physical toll but it also gave his life a finale which made it much easier for him to die.

With his body donated to medical science, Charlie had no funeral. A hundred people attended the memorial service that Julia and his closest comrades organised. Julia spoke tearfully about the loss of a great friend and mentor. Many others spoke: academics involved in his PhD, unionists who had worked on the trams with him, other unionists whose struggles he had supported, ex-Party members, community activists and relatives from his dead partner's family but none from his own—

Personal torturer

She must have drifted off. Frank was shaking her. Where was she? Her hands kneaded the soft material of the armrests.

'Come on, Julia,' he said, his voice croaky, his throat raw from vomiting. 'Time for bed.'

The residue of reminiscence dulled her mind. But the dinner party and Frank's appalling behaviour weren't easily forgotten. She was about to berate him for ruining her evening when she remembered the book Rogerson had given her. The note was still in her lap. When she realised it she sat up abruptly and tried to conceal it between the covers of the book without Frank noticing.

'What's the note about?'

'The note?' Julia's voice was brittle. 'Oh, nothing. Came with the book. A kind of review.'

Frank noticed the cover. '*Infinite Jest*. Who gave you that to read? Your personal torturer?'

She gaped at him unable to respond.

'Ah, I've guessed right,' he mumbled although struggling to keep his eyes open, interested solely in getting to bed. 'Come on.' He took her arm and helped her out of the armchair.

'I'll promise you one thing, Frank,' she muttered as they hobbled together towards the bedroom. 'Since it's your birthday tomorrow and today's Charlie's anniversary, I'll refrain from mentioning your totally embarrassing behaviour—how you ruined my dinner party. But we need to talk—about everything—about us, Frank—what's become of us, okay? Stop groaning, I'm serious. Let's just get to bed and sleep this off. So, not tomorrow, Frank. The day after.

Fateful day begins – minor preparations

Frank was up before her in the morning. It didn't matter what time he went to bed, he always rose at the same time each day, which went a long way towards explaining what happened to their ardour. She begrudged waking alone. Mostly they no longer had sex but, even so, his disappearance each morning felt like she was living a series of unconsummated one-night-stand debacles. There was nothing she wanted more than to wake next to the man she loved, cuddle him, sometimes fuck him, linger—loiter—together, start the day as a couple. She felt bereft. Usually during the week he returned to the bedroom to wake her with an irritating cheerfulness, like a ward nurse working to a busy schedule. Some weekends he didn't bother. Mercifully this weekend was one of them.

But she was woken by someone yelling outside. It sounded like their annoying neighbour, a retired doctor, who lived by himself and found fault with everything and everyone, including Julia and Frank who had gone out of their way to make him feel welcome when he first shifted in, gifting him a mud cake she had baked herself and offering him a few useful tips on the neighbourhood, like what day the bins went out and where to buy a good coffee. Even enduring the occasional lewd innuendo, as if he'd interpreted the mud cake as a come-on, she was determined to maintain good relations. His loud remonstration was unintelligible to her but she considered it inappropriate so early in the morning.

She reached for her phone to check the time and noticed a reminder on its screen. Frank's birthday. She groaned. Birthdays had always been important to her. It was the one day of the year when you could really make someone feel special. Their day! But for a few years Frank had been saying it merely reminded him he was getting old. She couldn't accept birthdays meant little to him. She persevered through his late forties but the last few years he had been so ungrateful she resolved to overlook it in future to see how he reacted. The previous year it had been all but forgotten because of Charlie's death. She would have liked to give him a bigger celebration this year as compensation, but knew how he would react. Instead she would wish him a happy birthday without a fuss and pretend it was just another day. In baser moments she hoped this would upset him. If birthdays didn't matter to him, couldn't he still see how important they were for her? Her list of Frank's insensitivities and faults was growing. And now, on his birthday, she was planning to see another man.

It shocked her. Despite her discontent it struck her as doubly unfaithful. She lay on her back, her fingers entwined in her hair, tugging to cause some pain, blinking at the ceiling rose. She was ready to criticise Frank whose attitudes, when they were at variance with hers, she was beginning to consider weaknesses. But was she any better? She was probably worse, she thought, and began to regret what she was yet to do. Definitely a weakness, Rogerson. She couldn't prevent his image meddling with her thoughts. He had written *I'm in love*. It should have been enough warning. It was extreme. Too dramatic. It was not what she was prepared to offer or accept. She should have come to her senses and *run a mile* as her mother would have advised. But she had no intention of doing that. She slid a finger into the soft groove between her legs and gently toyed with her clitoris.

Her head ached from the wine. *Cliff Rogerson, you bastard! Why are you doing this to me?*

The climax came from nowhere. A lightning bolt on a sunny day. A rude precipitous reaction that left her wholly unsatisfied. 'Damn,' she muttered.

Floorboards near the front entrance squeaked. She guessed it was Frank returning from somewhere. Maybe he knew what the doctor was shouting about. She rose too quickly and had to steady herself as a wave of nausea threatened to create more housework. She hastened into the ensuite and vomited into the toilet bowl.

The shower was a respite, even with the water-saving rose that had been fitted during the drought years when the price of water skyrocketed, which deprived her of the heavy drops she longed for. She stood motionless beneath its softer spray and let it assuage her.

Gradually sobriety returned.

She soaped her body with a gentle skin lotion and took a razor from the soap rack to shave her armpits. On a whim she started shaving her pubic hair and found it unexpectedly erotic, if not the act itself, at least the purpose. Conscious of her age she was modest with her design, no fancy shapes and not completely bald, which would look geriatric on a woman her age. When she left the shower she trimmed the longer strands back further with nail scissors and stood before the mirror to review her handiwork. Feeling slightly ridiculous, she found herself imagining a tattoo down there somewhere, maybe an ornate dragon.

After she had put the scissors to their proper use, clipping her toenails, she donned a bathrobe and slippers, wrapped her head in a towel, and went looking for Frank to wish him happy birthday.

Happy Birthday

When he wasn't eating breakfast in the kitchen she went to check if he was in the study, which over the years had become his sanctuary, a place she increasingly avoided, respecting his need for solitude. Since his retrenchment, he spent hours every day attempting to write a novel, no doubt a thinly disguised memoir, as if his life held some significance. He was secretive about it, refusing her offer to read it, which she interpreted as a fear of criticism rather than a fear of revealing what he had written about her. She wanted to tell him not to be so insecure but she wasn't cruel and she knew how important his writing had become as a form of therapy or an escape from the world around him after the loss of his job. His ego had taken a pounding. His self-esteem was at its lowest ebb. His identity as a journalist, a writer, was in tatters. She withdrew her own library and stationery from the study and set up her laptop in the sunroom at the rear of the house, which she preferred to the study anyway, for its natural light and view across their back garden.

Seeing Frank hunched over his desk squinting at the computer, Julia was overwhelmed with pity. Everything meaningful in his life was confined to that tiny screen. It appalled her and convinced her she was justified in wanting more than their moribund relationship. It assuaged her guilt. She could barely bring herself to greet him.

She invited him to join her for breakfast but the rest of the morning at home passed in a blur with her mind possessed entirely by Cliff Rogerson.

Later she vaguely remembered thinking Frank had been looking at pornography and in the kitchen he had ranted about another terrorist attack overseas, which infuriated her, suspecting he was trying to sabotage her plans with the terrible reality of the world. But she had gone ahead and doggedly made him some ready-mix pikelets.

Never much of a cook and with her culinary enthusiasm exhausted on the dinner party, she could barely manage to flip the pikelets. But she felt obliged to make an effort. As she stared into the frying pan it occurred to her that if her dalliance with Rogerson became known this might be the last meal she cooked for Frank. Pikelets! The absurdity of it filled her with dread. She felt like crying.

They had grown up together, travelled together, seen the world, shared so much, knew each other's quirks and foibles, adjusted their habits and opinions to accommodate their partner, learnt from each other. They had become closer, more intimate than either of them could have thought possible when they first went out together. Could she toss it all to the wind, pages torn carelessly from a book in which she had lost all interest and no longer intended to finish?

When she placed the plate of pikelets before him Frank noticed her despair but said nothing, too afraid of where a question might lead.

'Happy birthday, my love,' she said.

Impulsively he reached beneath her bathrobe and squeezed her thigh.

Her reaction frightened him. She recoiled from his touch. He frowned at her but she avoided his eyes. She hastened to the stove and brandishing the carton began to pour more mixture into the fry pan. 'Eat up,' she said, mortified. 'Now this is open we have to finish it.'

She had leapt away from his touch as if he had violated her. But how could he know that their life together was coming to an end? There had been no announcement until her rejection of his touch had inadvertently made it obvious.

She brought another plate of pikelets to the table and sat down opposite.

'What are your plans for the day?' he said, mocking.

She observed him calmly, about to confess her desire to have an affair with Rogerson, but hesitating. There was no way back from such a move. Frank had guessed what was coming and looked so fragile and fearful that any courage she had abandoned her.

'This year I've taken you at your word,' she said. 'So I haven't arranged any celebrations for your birthday. I'll leave you alone. I'm spending the day out with a friend first and then my mother.'

She noticed the grimace he tried to cover with his hand.

'Your mother? Things are improving between you two then?'

'What are you looking so glum about?' she asked. 'I thought this is what you wanted.'

'It's the coffee,' he said. 'No sugar. I'm not glum. Who's the friend you're meeting?'

She looked away evasively towards the sunroom at the rear of the house. The moment was here. 'Oh, just a uni friend for a bit of revision,' she stammered. 'You wouldn't enjoy it. Helping someone with their thesis. Technical stuff. Nothing interesting.'

He interpreted the gender-neutral '*their*' as an attempt at concealment. 'That young bloke from last night?'

'Peter?' A name had not occurred to her. 'He's doing a PhD.'

He followed her gaze, hoping it might offer him a respite from the anxiety churning his stomach. 'Will that Professor What's-his-name be there?'

'George? Professor Petrus? No. Why?'

'Just curious. You seem to be spending a lot of time with him lately, that's all?'

'What are you getting at, Frank?' She turned to look at him, surprised by the innuendo, starting to laugh.

'Nothing.'

She took her plate to the sink and left the kitchen.

Strangely the misgivings she felt about her intentions disappeared with Frank's inquisition. Clarity swept through her mind like a southerly breeze. She strode back to her bedroom and lay down for a while to settle her breathing.

But this was ridiculous—readily looking for a justification for an act she knew would be hurtful if Frank ever found out.

She returned to the kitchen determined to tell Frank, to explain to him why she needed to have a fling with Rogerson and how that's all it would be. It needn't damage their relationship if they were open about it. The real threat was concealment.

Frank was doing the dishes.

When she saw him her courage failed again. Telling a man in an apron and up to his elbows in soap suds that she was about to have an affair with one of the diners whose dishes he had stacked in the dishwasher seemed pitiless and beneath her. Instead she joked about his domesticity which, in his jaundiced mood, he interpreted literally, missing the irony, reacting with some negative words that were lost in the muddle of her desire.

She threw up her hands and hastened back to the bedroom. She had to get out of the house before her courage failed completely.

A dearth of clean underwear

Despite the chill, with the approach of summer and the promise of warmer days, she chose a loose, brightly-coloured dress with grey tights. She also fetched some matching socks from a drawer and fossicked around in the bottom of a cupboard for her Doc Martins, which she hadn't worn for years. Once more it crossed her mind that she was trying for a youthful look and wondered if Rogerson would approve or find it distasteful and a tad desperate.

Fearful he would she changed her entire outfit to something more conservative, darker colours—safe to wear in Melbourne—keeping the Doc Martins with neutral socks and taking a red woollen coat, the only item she donned with any colour until, blushing, she fossicked in her underwear drawer and found the flimsy erotic knickers she intended to wear despite them being a gift from Frank, which she had never worn because it somehow seemed to contravene her feminist principles.

She hastily undressed again, removed her white cotton tails and slipped on the panties.

Makeup she kept to a minimum although she matched her lipstick to the coat and panties.

As she reached the front door her escape was thwarted by her bowels, which threatened to explode. She raced to the downstairs bathroom. But Frank was there plucking hairs out of his ears. *Fuck, this is karma*, she thought. 'Sorry!' With frenetic dexterity she removed her underwear as far as her ankles and, hitching up her coat, reversed over the seat before last night's dinner gushed forth, a merciless evacuation that left her groaning about the prawns she'd eaten the previous evening.

Frank recoiled at the stench but managed to make a joke about their intimacy. Then he noticed the red panties and started ranting.

Again the moment had come for confession but she was ashamed of the evidence, ashamed she had made a fatuous effort to look sexy for another man in panties she refused to wear for Frank. Under the circumstances a confession would be ruinous. In a panic she gave him a plausible explanation about a dearth of clean underwear before she hastened away in a flourish of faux levity.

It was a relief to get outside away from her own duplicity and Frank who, with his insecurities, was beginning to disappoint her. She inhaled deeply and cast a nostalgic eye upon their home, aware an emotion as tepid as disappointment could foreshadow the end of love.

At least no mention was made of Charlie. She should have been grateful for that.

The way things can go wrong.

Rogerson was waiting at the Lounge Lizard. He had found the café using Google Maps. On the table where he sat was a mauve motorbike helmet with red and black lightning stripes. He was wearing a leather jacket and matching pants with padded shoulders, elbows and knees. His boots were buckled halfway up his shins.

Absorbed in his smartphone he wasn't aware of her arrival. She watched him for a minute. His dark hair was greased flat, his goatee clipped neat. His frown of concentration, concave cheeks and receding hairline lent him an intelligent, rakish mien, which was probably a truer reflection of his character than the suave, considerate, sartorial husband he had presented at the dinner party. But the riding gear alarmed her. She realised now what *take you somewhere in the Dandenongs* meant. Surely he wasn't expecting her to climb on the back of a motorbike. She had never been on one and knew nothing about them. The prospect horrified her. She looked around and saw a large machine parked against the curb right outside the café.

'Tell me I'm mistaken about this,' she said without greeting him, her fingertips pressing on the table top opposite his seat. 'You're intending to take me through the Dandenongs on that thing?' She lifted one hand to point vaguely towards the street.

'Julia. You're late. I thought you weren't coming.' He held up his phone. 'About to text you.'

'Maybe I shouldn't have come.' Her voice was vibrating with indignation as she lowered herself onto a chair. 'You should have warned me. If you expect me to get on the back of that with you, boyo, you've got another think coming.'

His smile was ingenuous, his gesture defensive. 'Wait, Julia, wait. Please. Just stay calm about it. I really wanted to give you a surprise. Have a coffee and just relax. What will it be? Macchiato?'

He looked around for the waitress but she was serving some-one outside. 'I'll get it, just sit there.'

While he was at the counter she tried to calm down and figure out what to do. Her mind was in turmoil. And how had he known what her favourite coffee would be? He must have watched her every moment at the weekend retreat. Her stomach was churning once more. This day was difficult enough without this unforeseen complication.

When on his return he kissed her cheek she flinched. 'This was a bad idea coming here. The staff know me and Frank. Don't give them a reason to gossip, Cliff, please.'

'You chose this place,' he said, sounding miffed. He slumped onto his chair and looked at her with one eyebrow raised, waiting.

'What sort of bike is it? A Harley?' With her accusation came a raised chin and haughty stare.

A strained smile contorted his goatee. 'A Harley? No, no, God, no. They're tractors. Mine's a Guzzi. A Le Mans Moto Guzzi. An eight-fifty. Classic Italian machine.' Seeing her disdain, he checked himself. 'But I know what you mean.'

Julia rolled her head back and put a hand on her forehead. 'Sorry, sorry. I'm hung over, I think.'

Her coffee arrived. She took a sip. No Sugar. She squeezed her eyes shut and puckered her lips. Its bitterness was restorative. 'You hear about these guys who have a mid-life crisis going out and getting a Harley to prove they've still got what they probably never had in the first place.'

'I've been riding since I was twenty. I'm not trying to recapture anything.'

'I'll take your word for it. All the same, I've never been on a motorbike in my life and I don't intend to start today.'

'You have no idea what you're missing.'

'I value my life too much to get on one of those things.'

'You go through the Dandenongs on a motorbike and your life will never be the same.'

'Oh, give me a break, Cliff. Anyway, look at me, look at how I'm dressed. It ain't motorcycle gear if you hadn't noticed. And wouldn't I need a helmet?'

'I didn't come empty handed, Julia. I've got an extra one with me and some gear you'll be able to pull under the skirt. That coat will be okay. What shoes have you got?'

'Doc Martins.'

'Perfect.'

'No, mate, no.'

'Please! You'll love me for it.'

'Is that what it takes?'

He stared at her for a moment. 'God, I want to fuck you like I've never fucked anyone before.'

'Why don't we just do that then? Forget the preliminaries.'

'Ah, but the ride, that's the aphrodisiac.'

'For you maybe.'

'Come on, Julia, try it. I guarantee you won't regret it.'

'Have you ever seen a male on the back of a bike with a female rider?'

'Well, as a matter of fact, that's how I fell in love with bikes. I used to have a girlfriend who took me around on hers.'

His wife's scars came to mind. 'Sarah?'

'No, not Sarah. Lovely Martha.'

'What happened to Martha then?'

He hesitated. 'She was too fond of taking all sorts of other guys around on the back of her bike.'

Her laughter rippled across the café, attracting the attention of its customers who couldn't help but reciprocate mildly, lightening the mood in the room despite the early hour.

Julia hid behind her mug of coffee, her eyes darting around looking for familiar faces, hoping to see none. 'Oh my God,' she murmured.

'What?' Rogerson looked around following her gaze.

'Outside at that table there. Frank's just turned up. I should've realised that might happen. But he *never* comes here on a Saturday morning!'

'You don't want him to see you with me?'

'No, of course not! I told him I was helping Peter Harding with his thesis.'

Rogerson tried hard to suppress a triumphant smile. 'I'll tell you what we'll do,' he said. 'I'll go out. He won't notice me. And I'll bring in the gear. You can put it on in the toilet here. Slip on the helmet before we go out. He won't recognise you.'

It happened that way except her stop in the toilet took longer than anticipated. She had pulled on the baggy canvas trousers, which easily fitted over her tights, and was tightening the waist cord when another rush of diarrhoea forced her out of them.

'A problem?' Rogerson asked when she finally emerged.

'How's *your* stomach?'

'Fine.'

Her face was ashen.

'Nerves?'

'Last night's prawns more like,' she said, lifting the full-face helmet over her head. 'Let's get out of here,'

As it confined her face she could smell a fragrance, maybe a residue of shampoo from the hair of his wife, Sarah, or some other woman. She had to allow Rogerson to strap it under her chin. Her misgivings and anger returned. How had she agreed to this?

He took her hand and led her from the café and across to his bike, passing close to Frank who was reading a newspaper, unawares.

'I get on first. Then, see that peg, put your foot on that and hoist yourself over the seat behind me.'

'It's hardly a fucking seat.'

'Here's some gloves. Put them on.'

Once she was gloved he manoeuvred her arms around his waist. 'Hold on.'

The acceleration startled her. It had her clutching for his leather jacket, her knees rising towards his armpits, one hand flying upward. 'Fuck!'

'Hold tight,' he yelled as an approaching car braked to avoid a collision.

By the first intersection she had hold of his sides, but as he went around the corner she resisted the tilt, tried to stay perpendicular as he leant the bike towards the curb. It forced him to correct his trajectory. Once he had straightened he proceeded with caution through some inner suburban streets to the Eastern Freeway, where he steadily increased his speed until he was a safe distance from other vehicles, hoping this would help Julia settle into the rhythm of the machine.

After her initial panic she tried to ignore her sense of vulnerability. The helmet was claustrophobic and it seemed to restrict her vision to a few degrees either side of its narrow opening. She had a primate grip on the waist band of his jacket. But once they were on the freeway she felt safer. There were no tight curves, plenty of space, a smooth surface, although she was buffeted by the air.

Reassured somewhat, she was by no means calm. She was furious with Rogerson for taking advantage of Frank's arrival, which had muddled her judgement and allowed her to be manipulated, a simmering fury against the impersonal leather-clad hulk to which she clung. And she had seen how close to a collision they'd come. He was arrogant and reckless, the archetypal biker. He could be any male. The desire she felt for him vanished into a state of impotence.

They had travelled to the end of the freeway and onto the tollway through the outer eastern suburbs when her bowels began to trouble her again. The few remaining shrimps were demanding a return to the ocean. Their exodus pressed painfully at the only outlet available. She willed herself to unclasp one hand from the jacket to thump Rogerson on the back. When he didn't respond, she shouted and thumped harder. 'I need a toilet stop!'

To hear her he leaned back, half-turning, which threw her off-balance. Her panic and lunging to hang on caused the bike to swerve across lanes. Rogerson managed to correct its trajectory and move into the emergency lane to stop. 'Sit still for Christ's sake, or you'll kill us both,' he said, his feet either side of his bike on the ground.

'Find me a fucking toilet!'

'Can't you wait?'

'Oh, God, Cliff! I can't believe I'm hearing this. Hurry! It's really fucking urgent!'

'All right. Hang on tight and don't throw yourself around.' He grabbed her hands and showed her where to grip his jacket. 'Don't let go.'

The pain doubled as Rogerson launched the bike into the flow of traffic. It eased somewhat when they reached cruising speed but intensified again as he took the next exit ramp with its tight curve.

There was a service station not far off the tollway. When the bike stopped Julia scrambled off and rushed into the toilet in time to avoid a major humiliation. She had struggled out of the riding pants Rogerson had lent her without a major mishap but her panties were soiled. Having lost their meaning she threw them into the sanitary napkin disposal bin. With them went her fantasy of his fingers on the silk. She washed her hands and removed her helmet.

In the mirror she looked at her frazzled face.

Her hair was plastered to her skull like scarecrow straw. Her eyes were bloodshot, the lids inflamed. Except for a few blotches on her cheeks and a reddish band where the helmet had pressed against her forehead, all colour was gone from her face. It was as if her frayed nerves had surfaced to drain her skin of its vitality. She looked middle-aged and sickly like a chronic convalescent. She looked sexless.

Leaning with both her hands against the vanity basin she closed her eyes and tried to regain some composure. She could hardly believe how rapidly her day had descended into a terrifying farce. She wanted to escape. She wanted to abandon Rogerson. She wanted to let him know his conduct was unforgivable.

She was furious with him and even more furious with herself. But her fury was rapidly becoming indiscriminate. She berated herself for her stupidity, for allowing her life to stagnate, which had led to her current predicament. She berated Frank, her colleagues and friends for failing to prevent it happening. She knew how unfair this was but she indulged her indignation anyway. It fortified her against the depression that rolled along the edge of her consciousness like an approaching cyclone.

Rogerson was talking bikes to a couple of young men who had wandered over after he had parked away from the bowsers. 'Ah,' he said as Julia arrived at his side with the riding pants under her arm and helmet in her hand.

The two enthusiasts noticed she was anything but relaxed. Anticipating an awkward scene one of them said, 'We'll be off then.'

'Yeah, nice talking to you,' said Rogerson, wistfully watching their departure as if their company was preferable to the impending encounter with Julia.

'Here,' she said, thrusting the riding gear towards Rogerson. 'I won't be needing these anymore.'

'What do you mean?'

'I'm not going any further, Cliff. I can't. I'm not blaming you. This was my mistake. Just go. Enjoy your ride. I'll find my own way home.'

'Julia, please! I'm only doing this for you.'

'No you're not. You're doing it for yourself. To impress me. If it was me you were concerned about you would not have railroaded me into it. I told you I didn't want to do it.'

'I wanted it to be a surprise. I thought you'd love it. Then Frank showed and we had little choice. You didn't want him to see us together, did you?'

'No. And that's my fault. That's why I'm trying hard to not get angry with you.'

'I really thought you'd love it,' he repeated.

'Bullshit, Cliff. You knew I'd be frightened. You'd get a kick out of it. What a tough guy you are. It's all about power. Your power over me. I can't respect you anymore. I'm sorry. Just go.'

She held out the riding gear. Rogerson stared at her as if he couldn't comprehend what she was saying. 'No, no, no, Julia, you've got it all wrong. Please, listen to me.'

When he failed to take the gear she placed it on the bike seat and began to walk away towards the road, although she had no idea what she would do next. There must be a bus that would take her to a station.

'Wait, Julia! Forgive me. Please! The last thing I wanted to do was upset you.'

She made the mistake of glancing back. The abject expression, the slumped shoulders, the movement away from his bike, as if he too was prepared to abandon it, his vulnerability to her wrath gave her pause.

She stopped but didn't turn. Instead she took in the surroundings as if noticing them for the first time: the comings and goings of cars, people at the bowsers, oil stains on the tarmac, the acrid smell of petrol, the two young men who were emerging from the shop through a sliding door, glancing her way and moving towards a late model ute, their sympathy with Rogerson.

'All right,' he pleaded. 'So I've got a problem, a macho problem maybe. Yeah, I did want to impress you but *not* frighten you. I was hoping it would be so exhilarating you'd get really turned on. When we make love—no wait, don't scoff—when we make *love*, I want it to be the best *ever* for both of us. I really do. You don't understand. I'm head over heels. That's never happened to me before. No bullshit. I can't explain it. I don't even want to try. Please Julia. Listen to what I've got to say.'

Her shoulders motioned indecision. For a moment she scanned the road in both directions, looking for a bus, before she turned to face him. His despondent eyes flickered with sincerity.

It shocked her to see his remorse, his love. She hadn't expected either. Love wasn't the emotion she was seeking. Her preoccupation was passion, or the lack of it, in her life. The thought that she might die without ever really experiencing it again depressed her more than most things. Rogerson was her best hope. She had felt the electricity between them the moment she set eyes on him. But the fiasco with the motorbike had ruined her plans. Yet here he was, prepared to admit his error, desperate for her to forgive him, in love, forlorn, pitiful.

 Uncharacteristically she was flattered.

She hated to think she was the cause of someone else's suffering. Against her better judgement she crossed to Cliff and kissed him, her tongue seeking pleasure through his yielding teeth.

A few people at the bowsers noticed, drawing hoots and whistles.

'What can we do?' His voice was full of hope. 'Julia, Julia.'

'I'll get back on the bike on one condition.'

He looked amazed. 'Whatever you say.'

'You take me back, slowly, carefully, into the city or Carlton or somewhere. We'll find something to do. An art gallery, a movie—something. Then afterwards, maybe, a hotel. What do you say?'

She didn't give him a chance to answer but kissed him again, a tender brush of his lips.

'Are you sure you don't want to see the Dandenongs?' He feigned a serious expression and then offered a feeble chuckle. 'Just joking, honest. Want some lunch? There's a restaurant just over there. Let's see if it's open.'

At a simple timber table in a quiet corner they ate agnolotti and drank the house wine while Rogerson talked about his life. A boy from country Victoria he had come to Melbourne to study, completing an economics degree and an MBA. For several years he worked for a financial corporation where he was involved in currency trading. It took him to Hong Kong, New York and London. Then once on a stopover in Singapore he met Sarah at a Changi Airport Bar. It was the beginning of an intense, erratic relationship. They wed at a city registry and shifted into a luxury apartment in the Eureka Tower, but when she became pregnant they bought a Victorian mansion in Hawthorn. Three children were born within five years, one of them dying early, a cot death, the others cared for by nannies.

His success as a financial advisor left him wealthy, but increasingly he became disillusioned and bored. He returned to study which soon led to a PhD and the position he now held at Monash University. There was enough status attached to his new career to keep Sarah happy, but long before he started shunning the pecuniary values that were important to her she was having affairs. When he discovered her infidelities she suggested he follow her example. He began his own.

'Our marriage is a charade, Julia.'

The way he told it his story demanded sympathy. She held his hand and grimaced. 'Mine's not,' she reminded him. 'Not yet, at least. I'll be frank with you, Cliff, and that's with a small *f*. All I really hoped for with you is what my girlfriends call a fling. They recommend it as a restorative. A cliché, I know. But now you're using words like *love*. That freaks me out.'

'Why have you procrastinated then if that's all you're after? You sent me away at the retreat which was the perfect opportunity for a fling, as you call it.'

'I got cold feet. I have a conscience too, you know. The last thing I want is to hurt Frank.'

'So you suffer yourself instead.'

'Maybe.'

'So a woman again suffers for the sake of her man.'

Julia looked at him intently. 'Yeah, you're right.'

'Frank need never know.'

'That's what I'm hoping.' Julia closed her eyes and shook her head, wondering if what she said implied consent. 'Can I ask what happened to Sarah? The enormous scar?'

'She jumped off a second storey balcony and landed on a fence. Thought she could fly. I think she was on LSD.'

'Let's go back.'

5 Julia

— Frank? What is this?

— What's what?

— This nonsense I found in your study.

— You shouldn't be going through my stuff.

— Since when have we not shared everything?

— Okay then, where did you spend the weekend?

— I told you I was staying at Mum's.

— I rang your mother. She was evasive. I asked for you. I got the distinct impression you weren't there.

— You know what she's like. Anyway, she told me about your call. You woke her. She was cross with you.

— Your phone was off.

— I was sleeping.

— On your own?

— Oh, I see where this is going. And it explains this nonsense you've been writing. Honestly, Frank, I'm really disgusted with you. You're pathetic.

— It's just some notes. I scribble down ideas for stories. Don't take any notice of them.

— Yes, I will. I have every right to since they're about me! What makes you think I was with Cliff Rogerson, of all people?

— I saw you. Outside the Nova. In the foyer at Brunetti's. You fondled him.

— You were there outside the Nova?

— Yes.

— And I fondled him?

— Ruffled his hair.

— Oh yeah, I did. I've wanted to do that for a long time. The moment arose after some silly joke he told about hair. No, not about your baldness, not everything's about you. So what? You know I'm demonstrative with my friends. It's never bothered you before.

— You weren't that demonstrative with him at the dinner party. The presence of his wife had something to do with that, did it? What were you doing there with him anyway?

— It was a coincidence, Frank. Most people we know regularly go to the Nova. I was there with Mum. She wanted to see the Judy Dench movie. He was there with Sarah. They were going to see that Korean film. It's a sensible way to recover from a night of heavy drinking, which is what we did, remember? You? Me? All the guests? Remember?

— Neither your mother or—what's her name?—Sarah?—was there. I watched you.

— Spying now, are you? Christ, what's gotten into you, Frank?

— Well?

— They *were* there. Maybe they were ordering cakes and coffee. Yeah, that's right. Mum wanted to pay for ours. She went into Brunetti's with Sarah. It was busy. They took a long time. Cliff and I stayed outside. That's when he told his joke. What did you think was going on? No, don't tell me, it's all here in these disgusting notes—here, look— you've got me jerking him off on a beach—after witnessing this one innocuous scene at Brunetti's! When was this—this lewd act supposed to have happened? Talk about drawing a fucking long bow! You know what this is, Frank? It's that porn you watch. It's ruined your imagination. And here listen to this *The easiest thing in the world for me would be to let you have your way with me.* That's just really bad, bad writing, something out of Mills and Boon. It's worse than *Fifty Shades.* If that's any indication of the quality of your prose, forget it, mate! Don't waste your twilight years.

— My twilight years? Please! Anyway it was your suggestion to write about sex. You said to put plenty of it into anything I write if I wanted to make money.

— Oh, for God's sake, can't you see it was a cynical comment about what's read these days. What's happening to you, Frank? I would never have had to explain that to you once. You would have got it. And we would've laughed together. We don't laugh anymore.

— Please try to understand, Julia, this is not about you. I want my novels to be about the crises facing ageing males in this heartless world. Men facing redundancy. Men whose youthful hopes and dreams have withered away. It's bound to touch on sex. I'm bound to draw on my own experiences and, by default, like it or not, the experiences of those around me. But it's intended to be allegorical. Anyway, what you've read are just sketches–ideas I might or might not use. Of course, later on down the track, once I've completed a reasonable draft I'll consult you as I've always done, darling, on matters that involved both of us. I can change those Mills'an'Boony bits. I'm not saying you'd have any editorial control, but naturally–

— You're accusing me of having an *affair*, Frank! What's allegorical about that? It's totally unwarranted and hurtful. What will our friends think? That I've been lying to them?

— They won't think it's you. They'll realise it's fictional.

— No they won't. You're using my bloody name!

— These are only notes. I can change that.

— You better! If you're going to write crap like this, if you're thinking of turning this–this *pornography*–into a book, please don't use *my* name or the names of *my* friends like this, because if you do, I won't be around for much longer. I'll go off and fuck Cliff Rogerson or someone just to spite you and it *won't* be allegorical then, I can tell you.

6 Frank

I'm sitting alone in my study. A work of art can be a solitary pursuit often with unpredictable consequences. The house is quiet again. Julia is away at her mother's. She has a few issues she wants to work through without my assistance. We are changing, the two of us, in ways I would never have foreseen. Physically we've become two different creatures. In no time at all she has become haggard. Lines have appeared at the corners of her mouth and around her eyes. There are smoky streaks through her hair. And the wine she drinks has brought rosacea to her cheeks. In the mirror I hardly recognise myself. I have a fixed perception of Frank Munro which must date back to my late thirties when I still had a reasonable head of hair and not an ounce of fat. Modesty aside for the moment, I was quite good looking with fine bone structure, a sensual mouth and eyes that radiated confidence and geniality, the sort of face that people warmed to instantly. I keep a photo from that era in my drawer as a reminder. Perhaps I shouldn't. My hair is almost gone. I'm left with a greying band above my ears that seem more salient than ever, whose rims are encrusted with sun-damaged weals that look like turrets along the ruins of a castle. Those eyes, now red and drooping with blepharitis, radiate trepidation and uncertainty. And that's just the head. I haven't got the will to go into details of my body's evolution. Suffice to say my reflection is another person, someone I wouldn't warm to immediately or go out of my way to get to know.

Once, Julia and I talked everything through. Now we hardly communicate at all and only when I take the initiative. For the sake of art I continue to write the story. I should have changed the names but Julia's threat was an affront not simply to me but to all writers, who should never be asked to compromise. Our quest is Truth. But she challenged that too. What I was writing was bullshit, she said. Even my character-isation of Charlie was inaccurate, insisting my friendship, my connection to him, had been circumstantial, episodic and probably opportunistic, which rendered my judgment unreliable. As far as she could see I no longer had friends at all because sustaining friendships required some effort. When for instance had I ever organised a dinner party? Or a picnic? Or a bushwalk? Or an evening at the cinema? It was always others who invited me. And without some attempt at reciprocation on my part one by one they had given up on me. Any friendships I had, if I insisted on calling them that, were maintained solely to serve my fiction. Charlie was not this incorruptible heroic socialist I had made him out to be. Yes, he was a warm, intelligent, compassionate bloke, who deserved praise for his community activism, but he was as solipsistic as the rest of us. He neglected his health because he was convinced his concerns should only be for the work-ing class and nothing individual, nothing personal, nothing remotely vain that might be construed as bourgeois by his enemies, who were far more numerous on his own side of politics than the other. Given the development of world affairs over the last few decades, nobody was remotely threatened by his ideology. The focus of Western intelligence agencies had shifted elsewhere. He should have taken more care of himself, gotten treatment earlier and he might still be alive today. It made Julia angry. He hadn't given himself a chance. And here I was, the opposite, but just as bad according to her, a self-serving, insecure individual with no convictions except this fixation on writing, in pursuit of the Truth, well, that was a laugh, scared of reality, scared of growing old, scared of the future. I was such a disappoint-ment to her. She needed time away from me to consider whether there was any point continuing our life together. The only positive she could draw from recent events was that I was unlikely to find a publisher.

Perhaps when that one occasion arose to get on more familiar terms with Chloe Dukakis, the time when we were alone at work and she had said *Oh, Frank, I don't know what to do*, her plea for me to step into her life—perhaps I should have taken it. For Julia's sake as well as my own.

My thoughts have a tendency to depress. Alone in this house I have no distractions. Even the television fails to induce its usual fugue. And for some reason the pornography I occasionally watch reminds me of death. At the back of my mind there's a graveyard ledger. There is Charlie, of course, but before Charlie my parents, before them my grand-parents, Julia's father, Julia's brother, most of my aunts and uncles, five cousins (one of them just a few days ago), one niece, two nephews, other friends and acquaintances, the parents and siblings and even the children of friends and acquaintances, a few of the local shopkeepers, several journalist colleagues, one or two neighbours and there's a startling long list of public figures from the political and entertainment worlds, each death a reminder that it is only a matter of time. And somewhere amongst them is Charlie's ghost.

Depression has a physical sensation, a clamp on the nape of my neck, pressing down, endeavouring to force my head between my knees, a debilitating weight, almost unbearable. For some suicide is the obvious remedy but not for me. Its promise is what terrifies me. Oblivion. My psyche screams out against it.

Feeling the panic that always looms when my thoughts drift into existential territory, I leave the PC, grab my laptop, jacket and karakul, check taps, lights and appliances and head for the door. I have to work on my novel but not at home, not while its emptiness is haunting me. There's only one place for me. Then it strikes me like a lightning bolt—there's no other way to explain it—years have passed since I've helped others. Julia is right. What a selfish bastard I've become. What's happened to my compassion? I'm no better than the doctor next door. Probably worse. This must be why she's leaving me.

It's such a terrifying epiphany that I hasten through the house to the sun room where Julia keeps her paperwork and I find a petition she's started. About a tunnel for a new toll road going right under a neighbouring suburb. Already it has dozens of signatures. The least I can do is gather some more on my way through the city. It's a good cause after all. Then another epiphany. No, stop. I'm a writer. An artist. We have our own way of doing things. I toss the petition back on her to-do pile.

As I reach the station the train arrives. The usual scene greets me. Passengers are hooked up to their smart phones, earplugs and tiny screens blocking out banal reality. We settle aboard. The stations come and go. Coburg. Moreland. Anstey. Brunswick. Jewel. Royal Park. Flemington Bridge. The train creeps around the curb into Macaulay. There is no-one on the platform. No ghost. No longer even the sensation of Charlie. He's gone. A gust of wind blows dust into the air. This residue of life is the best we can hope for.

Before we reach the CBD I decide to check my emails, hoping Julia might have sent me a reassuring note. Instead, to my astonishment, there is one from Dukakis. I open it. *Frank, hope you're enjoying your retirement. Listen, I've given your idea for a series on contemporary youth some thought. It's not a bad one and we're going with it. However, don't take this personally, I've given it over to a young team, a couple of our Gen Y-ers, who'll be closer to the subject matter, if you get my drift. It'll give them a chance to spread their wings. Maybe you should think about something closer to your own generation, on the baby boomers perhaps, although I know it's a bit passé and has been done to death already. Still, if you come up with a new angle, do slip me a reminder. Keep in touch. Dukakis.*

Nothing about hats. Nothing about catching up.

In the city I head north along Swanston Walk through the bustle of citizens attending to their ritual of shopping. There are touts and buskers and beggars on the footpath under neon signs. Every shop has a sale. One sale after another. Eternal sales. Only the name changes. Boxing Day Sale. Stocktake Sale. End of Financial Year Sale. Closing Down Sale. Relocation Sale. Bullshit Sale. I want to spread my arms in a gesture of despair and rebellion. I want to shout, *Do any of you believe this bullshit?* But I don't shout. I'm a writer not a protester. Not a commie as the good doctor called me. As I try to push through the throng, clutching my laptop, I'm met with resistance. *Get out of my way, fatso,* a similarly-shaped, junk-food addict mutters. I cast my eyes towards the litter underfoot, mostly the disposable containers from fast-food joints careful of my step, putting distance between my insecurities, my doubts and the future. I'm a writer. Forget about Julia. Forget about all the others, at least until the book is finished.

The State Library has always been my (our) refuge, a grand old colonial building with stately ionic columns, opposite Melbourne Central at the corner of La Trobe Street. Near the footpath is a sculpture, a postmodern piece that looks like a fragment of another library, a cornice rupturing the earth, as if, with a diligent archaeological dig, another edifice could be found beneath, a vast subterranean store of forgotten literature.

Glad to leave the street I enter the real library reverentially, pass through its refurbished section, which is full of computers and white light, and up the stone stairs to the old octagonal reading room with its walls of books and massive dome. It is as quiet as a mausoleum, and in a way that describes its function: a resting place. For ideas. Charlie's thesis is in here somewhere. I circle anticlockwise, my hand out touching the spines of books. I stop and remove a tome at random from the wall. It's weighty. It has substance. It's a corpse. A mummified corpse. And like all corpses it is testimony to years of living, working, thinking. I want my book, if I ever finish it, to end up here so it will outlast me. I've always felt that this is the place where I could belong.

There are scholars, researchers, autodidacts, writers, bored retirees, street people, lost souls and bookworms seated at the desks that radiate from the central podium. It's here that Julia would sometimes come to work on her PhD, one which was published and would be on a shelf here somewhere too. She talked about how much she loved this room, sitting amongst learned people while she learned. She, too, felt that she belonged here.

Before I settle down to the writing I decide to view the scene from above. There are tiers built below the dome, three galleries where you can look down upon the desks at the readers and writers. I take the lift and stairs to the top level to view the peaceful scene. It is like a sanctuary from the madness outside, the earthly travails, conflict, war, terrorism, work, the daily grind, shopping, begging. I lean against the balustrade and look across the void, absorbing the tranquillity. There are other observers at different points around the gallery and I notice a couple in one alcove who seem as moved by the ambience as I am. They kiss, a lingering embrace, that stirs some yearning in me. I watch them wishing the moment could last forever. But I know it will be fleeting. It is only after they part and turn to look into the air between us that I recognise one of them. It's Julia in the low-cut crimson dress I've seen her in before. The other, whose identity is obscured by a shadow, gently places a hand upon her shoulder. Julia's face is radiant as her eyes rise to observe the dome and linger on its purity.

An inaccessible space.

As if its quality is too much to bear she lowers her gaze and sees me.

No, no, no. Better—

They kiss, a lingering embrace, that stirs some yearning in me. I watch them wishing the moment could last forever. But I know it will be fleeting. It is only after they part and move away that I notice Julia. In an adjacent alcove. Standing alone. Her face is radiant as her eyes rise to observe the dome and linger on its purity.

An inaccessible space.

As if its quality is too much to bear she lowers her gaze and sees me. After her initial surprise she gives me an ambiguous smile.

Then she, too, is gone.

The alcove is empty.

www.ingramcontent.com/pod-product-compliance
Lightning Source LLC
Chambersburg PA
CBHW021015120726
47905CB00009B/3025